W9-CBN-107

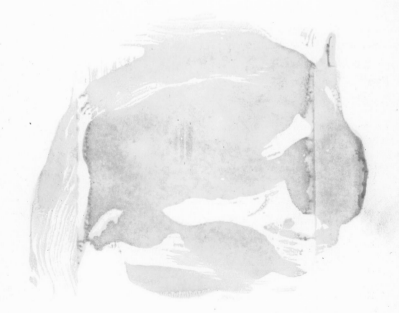

MENDELE MOCHER SEFORIM

The Travels and Adventures of
Benjamin the Third

SCHOCKEN BOOKS · NEW YORK

Translated from the Yiddish by Moshe Spiegel

First SCHOCKEN PAPERBACK edition 1968

Second Printing, 1975

Copyright © 1949 by Schocken Books Inc.

Library of Congress Catalog Card No. 49–9256

Manufactured in the United States of America

TABLE OF CONTENTS

INTRODUCTION   7

PREFACE   9

   I *Who This Benjamin Is, His Beginnings, and How He Hit upon the Idea of His Travels*   15

  II *How Benjamin Became a Martyr — and Zelda a Deserted Wife*   23

 III *Benjamin Joins Forces with Senderel the Housewife*   34

 IV *Exodus*   46

  V *First Leg of the Journey*   51

 VI *Benjamin Comes a Cropper*   61

VII *Benjamin Upsets the Applecart*   68

VIII *How the Two Went Begging from Door to Door*   75

 IX *The Ancestors Intercede*   78

  X *"Hurrah, the Red Jews!"*   86

 XI *Wonder upon Wonder on Lake Pyatignilovka*   96

XII *Steam Baths — and Hot Water*   105

XIII *In the Toils*   116

XIV *Once a Bride, Again a Maid*   122

MENDELE MOCHER SEFORIM (Mendele the Book Peddler) is the pen name of Shalom Jacob Abramovich, one of the leading Hebrew and Yiddish writers of modern times. He was born in Kopyl, Lithuania about 1836, and died in Odessa in 1917.

The young writer's first concern was to further the education of East European Jewish youth in the spirit of the Haskalah, the anti-traditionalist enlightenment movement aiming at a "Europeanization" of Jewish life and letters.

This didacticism retreats to the background in his imaginative work, short stories and novels, in both the Hebrew (from 1863) and the Yiddish (from 1864). The collected works, seven volumes in Hebrew and twenty in Yiddish, provide a great panorama of Jewish life in Eastern Europe, and especially within the Pale of czarist Russia, in all its political and economic insecurity. Its symbol is the "Luftmentsh" and the homeless vagrant passionately pursuing his illusory goals. This Mendele sees with the eye of a satirist.

Benjamin the Third (first published in 1885) is a classical satiric picture of the unrealistic, narrow and day-dreaming life of the ghetto. Benjamin, who lives in a world of visions and grotesque idealism and who leaves the microscopic Tuneyadevka in his adventurous search of the legendary Ten Tribes, is shaped in a manner somewhat resembling Cervantes' Don Quixote. The subtly humorous story comes to an abrupt end, and it would appear that Mendele vaguely intended going on with it; but this intention was never realized.

By the way, our Benjamin is "the third" of the travelers of that name: the first being Benjamin of Tudela, the thirteenth-century Spanish traveler and author, the second being Joseph Israel Benjamin, who in the middle of the nineteenth century set out on his travels to the Orient and whose adventures carried him even to America.

After a long period of devotion to Yiddish writing Mendele returned to the Hebrew language. His best works in Yiddish he recast into Hebrew, among them *Benjamin the Third*. In both languages he was a literary pioneer; he created the Yiddish literary language and laid the foundation of modern Hebrew style, freeing the language from the bombast and archaism of the Haskalah period.

He is affectionately called *Der Zeide, Sava,* the Grandfather, of modern Yiddish and Hebrew literature. The great Jewish humorist Sholom Aleichem considered himself Mendele's grandson.

THIS IS Mendele the Book Peddler speaking.

Praised be the Creator Who fixes the destiny of the heavenly spheres and the fate of all His earthly creatures. Even the least blade of grass will not sprout unless some angel urge it on: "Grow, now! Come forth!" How much more so in the case of man, whom an angel most certainly must urge on: "Grow on! Come forth!" And still more with our praiseworthy little Jews. Among us no oaf dare open his mouth out of turn, a simpleton doesn't step into a sage's shoes, an ignoramus into a pietist's, a boor into a learned gentleman's, until such time as each oaf, simpleton, ignoramus and boor is goaded and urged on by some angel. It is likewise the angels who urge on our paupers of every sort, admonishing them: "Grow, ye poor, ye beggars — beggars born, beggars broken-down, plain-spoken and close-mouthed — sprout, spring up like grass, like nettles! Go ye forth, ye Jewish children — go ye begging from door to door!"

But that's not what I'm leading up to. What I'm leading up to, my dear friends, is how one of our brethren journeyed forth to far-off lands and won glory thereby. Stirring accounts of the noteworthy journey to lands somewhere far, far in the East, undertaken by one Benjamin, a Polish Jew, appeared last year in all the English and German newspapers.

"Just think!" people marveled. "Here's a Polish Jew, unarmed and without any means of transportation save shank's mare, with nothing but a sack over his shoulder and a prayer shawl and phylacteries under his arm, who made his way into regions that great and celebrated British explorers had never reached. Can it be that Benjamin attained his goal not by ordinary human powers, but by means of some power that the intellect cannot grasp? In other words, the intellect is just as powerless as power is unintelligible — "

However, no matter how the thing came about, the world is indebted to Benjamin for the marvels and phenomena that have been revealed through him, and which have changed the map of the earth. Benjamin fully merits the medal which the Geographical Society has bestowed upon him.

The Jewish newspapers, as their readers will readily recall, splashed the news of Benjamin's peregrinations over their front pages, all through last summer. They tabulated all the great in Israel, from Adam on, in order to confirm the sagacity of Israel. They also enumerated all the explorers, starting with Benjamin the First, who had flourished something like seven hundred years ago, and Benjamin the Second, down to the latest crop of globe-trotters of this day and age. And, in order to enhance the significance of our Benjamin's travels, after an old custom they minimized the contributions of the others and stated that the whole lot of present-day explorers amounted to no more than a band of miserable vagabonds who didn't know chalk from cheese, begging from door to door. All these were, assuredly, no more than apes as compared to Benjamin the Third, your only true and real traveler. And these papers, in commenting on him and the narrative of his journeys, came up with the old tag: "Never have such fragrant herbs sprung up in Israel before!"

Blessed and adorned with diamonds ought to be the one (they all said in one voice) who would delve into the great treasure-trove of Benjamin's travels, available in all foreign languages, and then expound it in the Holy Tongue, so that our brethren, too, might savor of the honey overflowing from the Jewish hive and rejoice therein.

And so I, Mendele, whose aim it has been all his days to do for his brethren all that was within his power and his ability, could restrain myself no longer, and I said to myself:

"Before the writers of Hebrew — whose little fingers are broader than my loins! — before they wake up to the task of rendering the narrative of Benjamin's travels into the Holy Tongue, let me try to give at least an abbreviated account of it in plain, everyday Yiddish."

So, despite my years and aches — may you be spared the latter — I girt my loins as if I were a giant, and attempted to gather from the great treasure things likely to interest the children of Israel, and to retell them freely, in my own fashion. Somehow I felt as though I were solemnly adjured from above: "Awaken, Mendele, and crawl out from your snug nook! Bestir thyself and gather handfuls of Benjamin's precious fragrant herbs, and prepare them into such viands as your brethren may delight in!"

And so, with God's help, crawl out I did, and I did as I had been bidden. Here, then, is the delectable repast, and may it prove, my dear friends, to your taste!

The Travels and Adventures of Benjamin the Third

"ALL MY days (so says Benjamin the Third himself) — until my great journey, that is — I have lived in Tuneyadevka [Droneville]. There I was born, there I was raised, and there I had the great good fortune to marry my spouse, the virtuous Zelda, may her days be long in the land!"

Tuneyadevka is a little town, far, far out in the hinterland, so far removed from the great world that whenever, once in a blue moon, some traveler does chance to come, all the windows and doors are flung wide and people swarm to gawk at the newcomer. Leaning out of their windows the neighbors ask one another: "Who can this stranger be? Where does he hail from? Why has he picked out our town, of all places? What's behind all this? Nobody's going to come here without a good reason! Something must be up; we've got to find out what's what!"

Whereupon each one becomes anxious to show his cleverness; conjectures of all sorts fly thick and fast. Old folks recall other strangers who had visited their town in the past, in such and such a year; the town wits are reminded of stories not quite decorous, at which the men stroke their beards and smile, and the older women rebuke the wags, not too seriously, while the young matrons turn their faces away, only to look back furtively and giggle. The surmises concerning the stranger make the rounds, picking up momentum and bulk like a rolling snowball, until they fetch up at the House of Prayer, just as every conceivable topic does, whether it has to do with family squabbles, the political problems of Stambul, Turkey and Austria, finance, Rothschild's fortune as compared to the fortunes of the leading local gentry and other Midases, rumors about government decrees, the legends of the Red Jews* and so on. A committee of local notables is always in session at the House of Study, throughout the day and far into the night, praiseworthily sacrificing not only their own interests but those of their families to the public weal, wholeheartedly devoting their attention to these public affairs, yet receiving no other award for their efforts save such as may accrue to them in the Hereafter. These matters are frequently transferred for further debate to the communal baths, where the elders, duly assembled, dispose of them, once and for all and irrevocably — for even if all the Kings of the East and the West were to view the verdict with disfavor, it wouldn't do them the least bit of good. The Turks once came mighty close to losing their realm at such a palaver — who knows what would have become of them if a few worthy citizens hadn't defended their interests? Rothschild, too, almost lost something like ten

* The Red Jews are identified with the Ten Lost Tribes of Israel whom "the King of Assyria . . . carried . . . away unto Assyria and placed . . . in Halah and in Habor, on the river of Gozan, and in the cities of the Medes" (II Kings 17:6).

16

to fifteen million rubles here. Several weeks later, however, the good Lord took pity on him and the bathhouse statesmen granted him, during a lively conference in the steam room, a clear gain of something like a hundred million rubles!

The denizens of Tuneyadevka are, God save us all, dreadfully poor. To tell the truth, however, they're a merry lot of poverty-stricken, devil-may-care optimists. Just ask a Tuneyadevka Jew (do it suddenly, however): "How do you get along?" He'll seem flustered, not knowing what answer to make at first, but on regaining his composure he'll answer you in all seriousness: "How do I get along, you ask? Ours is a kind Lord, I'm telling you, Who never forsakes His creatures! He supplies their needs and, I'm telling you, He'll go on supplying them!"

"Yes, but just what do you do for a living? Have you a trade of any kind, maybe, or a little business?"

"Praised be the blessed Name! I have — praised be the Lord — I have, sure as you see me, a gift from the Almighty — a musical voice. So, I'm the cantor during the High Holiday services in the settlements hereabouts. Now and then I perform circumcisions, and when it comes to perforating matzahs with the indented wheel, there's nobody like me. I also have a bit of luck once in a while as a marriage broker. I have a seat, as sure as you see me, in the synagogue. Then, too — just between you and me — I run a still that gives a little panther milk; I've also got a nanny goat — may she be spared the Evil Eye! — that's a good milker, and a well-to-do relative, not far from here, who likewise can be milked a little, whenever I'm really hard up. Aside from all these things, God is our father, I'm telling you, while the Israelites themselves are merciful and the sons of the merciful!"

Another thing to the credit of Tuneyadevka's citizens is that they're invariably satisfied with whatever God may send them and aren't too choosy when it comes to clothes or food. If your Sabbath gabardine, let's say, is shabby, frayed, torn and not too neat, it doesn't much matter, for wasn't the garment once made of satin? If your skin shows through the threadbare stuff as through a sieve, what of it? Is anybody going to stop for an inspection? And suppose your low shoes are down at heel and out at toe — what's the matter, aren't heels and toes as much flesh and blood as the rest of your body? When it comes to food — bread and soup (if you're lucky enough to get them) make a meal that's not at all bad. And if, of a Friday, you have a loaf of white bread and a dish of something stewed (if you can but afford them), they are verily a royal feast, the like of which is not to be found anywhere else in the world. Should any man tell them of delicacies other than stewed fish or meat, with carrots and parsnips by way of dessert, they would think him queer and would be likely to snicker and poke fun at him, as if he were cracked and were trying to take them in with a cock-and-bull story.

On the fifteenth day of the month of Shevat they nibble at a sliver of the traditional carob pod — there's a fruit for you! The sight of it reminds you of Jerusalem. More than once will the partaker thereof lift his eyes up to heaven with a sigh and murmur: "Merciful Father, lead us with our heads held high into our own Land, where even the goats feed on carob pods!"

Once, by pure chance, someone brought a date into Tuneyadevka. How the townfolk flocked to gape at it! On opening the Pentateuch someone discovered that dates were referred to in the Holy Writ! Think of it! Dates grew in the Land of Israel, actually! As they contemplated the date, a vision of the Holy Land spread out before them; here one crossed the Jordan; there was the Cave of Machpelah, wherein the patriarchs and the matriarchs are entombed, and the grave of our Mother Rachel; over there was the Wailing Wall; some bathed in the hot springs of Tiberias; others scaled the heights of the Mount of Olives; others still ate their fill of carob pods and dates, and stuffed their pockets with the sacred soil, ultimately to be placed in pillows under their heads in their graves.

The visionaries sighed and tears welled up in their eyes.

"In those days," Benjamin relates, "all of Tuneyadevka found itself in the Land of Israel — at least in the visions they conjured up. People were engrossed in talk of the Messiah. . . . The town's newly appointed Chief of Police ruled it with an iron hand: he had snatched the skullcaps off several Jews, cut an earlock from another, locked up several townsmen overnight for not having their passports with them; while from still another he had confiscated a goat merely because the animal had eaten all the straw from a neighbor's newly thatched roof. And it was because of him that the statesmen at the

House of Study were so fervently concerned about the status of Turkey: Until when would the Sultan exert his influence? One day their discussion turned to the Ten Lost Tribes, to the good life they undoubtedly led in their distant realm, secure in their dignity, weal and goods. Wonderful tales were related of the prowess of these legendary Red Jews, the *Bene Moshe,* or the Sons of Moses. Eldad ha-Dani, another great traveler, also contributed to the general excitement. It was the enthusiasm of those days that chiefly spurred me on to the journey I eventually undertook."

Up to this point Benjamin's state had been like that of a chick in its shell, or a worm in horseradish. He had a notion that the world's end lay just beyond Tuneyadevka; that life could nowhere be more comfortable than it was right here.

"I thought (so Benjamin tells us in one passage) that no one could wish to surpass our landlord in wealth. What a lavishly furnished household he had! Just think of it: four pair of brass candlesticks, a six-branched candelabrum surmounted by an eagle, two copper pots and at least five pans (likewise of copper), a shelf crowded with pewter plate, not less than a dozen tablespoons of German silver, two goblets of real silver, a Hanukkah lamp, an onion-shaped watch in a double case and with a thick chain of artificial pearls, all of two milch cows and a young cow that was about to calve, two Sabbath gabardines, and other such treasures. And I used to think that there was nowhere else so great a sage as our Reb Isaac David the son of Reb Aaron Yossele the son of Sarah Zlata. Why — no trifle, this! — it was rumored that in his youth he had actually studied *fractions!* He might have become a statesman, had luck favored him even a little. Who else, I mused, had so patriarchal a face, such engaging small talk, as our Heikel the Stammerer. Or who was so competent a medico as our own healer, who could revive the dead and who, so it was told, had acquired his medical lore from a gypsy — and not just any gypsy, at that, but a direct descendant of Egypt's ancient wizards?"

In a word, life in his home town seemed to Benjamin to be good and glorious, even though he lived in poverty and his wife and children went around in rags. However, had Adam and Eve been disconcerted by the fact of their being naked and barefooted while they were still in the Garden of Eden?

Nevertheless, the wonder-tales of the Ten Lost Tribes penetrated to his very heart, and thenceforth Tuneyadevka became too small to hold him; he felt drawn toward far-off regions, as the hands of infants are drawn toward the moon. What, at first glance, do a date, a police inspector, a skullcap, an earlock, a poor Jew apprehended late at night, a goat and a straw-thatched roof — really, what did they all amount to so far as Benjamin was concerned? Nevertheless, all these had left their impress upon him, eventually leading to his now celebrated journey. It's quite possible, of course, that Benjamin had been born with the spark of adventure in him. But that spark would certainly have died out if the wonder-tales and other influences of that period had not served to fan it to a blaze. And even if the spark had not been put out altogether, without the spirit of the time it would have smoldered to so little effect that Benjamin would have turned out a mere water carrier or, at best, a carter.

(I myself have met, during my lifetime, many a carter and teamster who could have made as great a traveler, I'm sure, as some of those now knocking about in our midst. That, however, is another of those things which I hadn't set out to tell you.)

From that time on Benjamin began most fervently to meditate upon Rabbah Bar Bar Hana's journeys over land and sea; later on a volume of Eldad ha-Dani's fell into his hands, as well as *The Travels of Benjamin* (the First), depicting that noted explorer's wanderings to the very ends of the world, some seven hundred years ago, and such books as *In Praise of Jerusalem* and *The Image of the World,* wherein the Seven Wisdoms and all the world's marvels, and all its strange and unique creatures and creations, are described in seven small pages. These works opened new horizons before him that affected him profoundly.

"Those wonder-tales fascinated me exceedingly. And how often did I cry out in my rapture: 'Would that the Almighty might but help me to see even a hundredth part of all this with my own eyes!' My fantastic visions bore me far, far away."

Thenceforth Tuneyadevka became too small to hold him. He made up his mind to throw off its trammels, break loose from its moorings, to escape, even as a chick escapes its shell, to catch his first glimpse of the fair world without.

OUR BENJAMIN was, by nature, an egregious coward. He feared to go out at night; you just couldn't get him to sleep in a room all by himself; going any distance from town unaccompanied was to him the same as risking his life, for — God forbid! — who could tell what might not befall! He was in mortal dread of the smallest cur.

"Once" — Benjamin tells us — "once, on a sweltering day, in the month of Tammuz — I remember it distinctly, as though it had happened this very day — our rabbi had gone for a dip in the lake on the outskirts of town. I and two of my friends trailed after him in awe, fully confident that in the rabbi's presence no evil could befall us, and that with God's help we should return home safe and sound. No small matter, this — the protection of a rabbi, to whose authority the whole world defers, who can have no superior, whose honorary titles alone fill an entire page! The rabbi preceded us at a leisurely pace, some distance ahead; however, just as he reached the lake and began to undress, a peasant boy appeared and sicked his dog on him. Whereupon the holy man, scared out of his wits, took to his heels, holding his — you'll pardon the expression — breeches up with one hand and clutching his round plush hat in the other. We boys were simply flabbergasted: if Leviathan himself was caught in the meshes, what were we minnows in the mud to do? We slued right around and, screaming with fright, dashed off swift as deer until, all out of breath, we reached town far ahead of our idol. And what a to-do and confusion there was, what shouts of 'Fire! Murder! Massacre!' "

Consequently when Benjamin (Benjamin the Third, to be precise) decided to undertake his journey to far-off lands, he vowed to cast off his cowardice and poltroonery. He mustered up courage enough to go out alone, precisely at night, to sleep in a room all by himself and, as often as he could, ventured out of town for solitary walks, though his health suffered and he was consumed with fear.

His odd conduct at home and in the House of Prayer, his pale, bizarre face, and his daily disappearances for hours at a time gave rise to a great deal of talk. The comments were, as always, many and varied. "Benjamin must be out of his mind," said some. "It can't be anything else. First of all, he always was daft — he has a screw loose. And, secondly, Tuneyadevka has been without a town idiot for some time — and isn't it written: 'Each town hath its sage, and each its idiot?' Particularly so during a heat wave, such as we're having right now. So, why couldn't it be that he has gone mad?"

But there were others, headed by Reb Isaac David the son of Reb Aaron Yossele, who moralized to the following effect: *"Teh, teh, teh* — and again *teh!* It's true that Benjamin isn't bright — very far from it. But from that it doesn't follow that he's mad, either. For the moot point arises: Why has he gone mad precisely now and not before? Furthermore, why not last summer, or the summer before that, when the heat was much worse? What's the inference, you ask? The inference is . . . well, take our lake, for instance. Our lake, as everybody knows, has claimed one life, annually, from time immemorial, and yet in recent years it hasn't claimed a single victim. On the contrary, the lake itself has dropped so low during the past few years that there are places in it where you can cross it practically dry-shod. But what's that got to do with Benjamin, you ask? Oh, what people!"

Most of the people, however — and the women were of the number — waxed eloquent: "Benjamin must be in cahoots with *Them* . . . with the Powers of Darkness. He must be hand in hand with . . . with the Evil One. If not, why does he go traipsing around by himself so late at night? Why does he sleep all alone out in the shed? Zelda, his own wife, hinted that she heard strange noises in the shed, at night, like footsteps — "

This controversy, as usual, came to the ears of the parliamentary group debating round the synagogue stove, and from there rolled on to the presidium at the bathhouse. Both chambers having failed to solve the matter, it was tentatively decided to form a committee of esteemed citizens, headed by the scribe of the Holy Scrolls, which was to scrutinize the text of the mezuzahs* of all Jewish houses. And since such a procedure was a communal affair, inaugurated for the public welfare, it was deemed advisable to subsidize this investigation by

* A small parchment scroll inscribed with biblical verses (Deut. 6 : 4–9; 11 : 13–21) and attached to the doorpost.

raising the tax on ritually slaughtered animals and poultry. Which bore out the aphorism current in Tuneyadevka: All talk inevitably ends up with the subject of death, and all communal discussion culminates in a further tax on meat. And, in truth (for such is the nature of things), any other course seemed unthinkable. Logic arrives at much the same conclusion: Death is the end of man, and taxes the end of the Jew. Death and taxes: the two unavoidable realities, never to be shaken off. Thus hath the Lord created the world, and as He created it so must it be, there being no alternative. Only heretics question such things.

It was shortly afterwards that a cer*ain event, whereby Benjamin became celebrated, took place.

One scorching day in midsummer he strolled out into the near-by woods, about three Sabbath limits* away. He carried along his books, without which, by that time, he never budged. Wearied by his prolonged ramble and absorbed in thought, he slumped down in the shade of a tree. There was more than enough to set him thinking. Before long his fancy carried him away to climes as far off as the world's end. He had visions of himself traversing mountains and valleys, trudging through deserts and stony tracts, all mentioned in his books. He followed the trail of Alexander of Macedon, of Eldad ha-Dani, and other such adventurers. He came upon the fearful Great Viper with its enormous hands, the Lindenworm, strange

* The Sabbath limit (the distance beyond which no Jew might go on the Sabbath) is 2,000 cubits, or roughly five-ninths of a mile. Benjamin's stroll thus was less than 1¾ miles.

26

reptiles, and all sorts of vermin and monstrosities. But he surmounted all obstacles unharmed and at last reached the Red Jews, the Sons of Moses, and talked with them face to face. . . .

Breaking off his reveries from time to time, he pondered how and when he was to set out on his great journey. Night came on as he sat there plunged in thought. He arose, stretched himself, and started for home. He walked on and on but saw no way out of the woods. He plodded along for an hour, two hours, three, four — but there was still no end to the trees. Thus he straggled still deeper into the heart of the forest — and by now the night was so dark that he might as well have been blind. To make matters worse, a tornado erupted with torrential rains and thunder and lightning, the trees bent and made weird noises. Benjamin halted, drenched to the skin, his teeth chattering from cold and the terrifying din. From moment to moment he imagined that a bear was about to pounce upon him, or that a lion or a leopard was poised to tear him to pieces; he felt sure he saw the Matul, that mythical dragon, whose paws are so enormous that it can toss an elephant about. He was in mortal fear, and famished on top of that, inasmuch as he hadn't tasted a morsel of food the whole day, save for a piece of a hard buckwheat cracker. Sunk in his misery, Benjamin fell to praying fervently, from the very depths of his heart.

Day, with God's help, broke at last, and our Benjamin resumed his plodding way. After considerable trudging he finally struck a narrow path. He proceeded along this trail for no more than an hour or two when he was surprised by the echo of a man's voice in the distance. This, however, brought but little joy to Benjamin, who recoiled in dismay. That voice, he reflected, could belong to none other than some murderous brigand. Trembling like an aspen leaf he took to his heels. But when he stopped at last, he soliloquized:

"For shame, Benjamin! You yearn to sail across oceans, to wander through deserts teeming with reptiles, wild beasts and cannibals, yet here you are appalled by the mere echo of some common cutthroat! Fie, Benjamin, you ought to be ashamed of yourself! Did Alexander of Macedon quit like you when he was flying on his eagle, and the gobbet of meat on the tip of his sword — with which meat he both lured the bird on and steered it — was gone? No! *He* did not quit. Alexander sliced off a chunk of his own flesh and stuck it on the sword! Courage, Benjamin — God doth but want to try thee. Think of the happy moment, Benjamin, when you shall have passed the trial. For then you will be a valiant man and deemed worthy by Him Whose Name is blessed to proceed to the *Bene Moshe,* to discuss with them the state of our local brethren. If you will but meet this one trial and turn back to that voice you hear, you will overcome all cowardice and fear and become a perfect instrument, a blessing to Israel, and an enhancement of the glory of Tuneyadevka. Tuneyadevka and Macedonia — two glorious places, destined to enjoy an equal fame, because of Alexander of Tuneyadevka and Benjamin of Macedon — or is it the other way around? . . ."

And so our Benjamin, imbued with great faith and enheartened, turned round sharply and went on until he caught sight of the brigand — an old muzhik driving a loaded cart drawn by a pair of oxen.

"Good day to you!" Benjamin greeted him, in a queer, spluttering voice. The salutation conveyed various things: it was both a wail of woe and a plea, as if to say: "Here I am — do with me what you will!" And, likewise: "Pray, be merciful to me, as well as to my wife and little ones at home!"

Having yammered out his greeting, Benjamin became inarticulate and felt a strangling and numbing sensation creeping over him. His head began to swim, everything dimmed before his eyes, his knees buckled and he keeled over.

When he recovered his senses he found himself sprawled out in the cart atop a huge sack of potatoes and covered over with the muzhik's overcoat of coarse cloth. Lying near his head was a trussed rooster that was regarding him malevolently and askance. The rest of the cart was filled with wicker hampers of garlic, onions and other farm produce. There must have been some eggs, too, for now and then the chaff in which they were bedded would fly right into his eyes. The muzhik leisurely puffed away at his cigarette of shag rolled in a scrap of newspaper, and kept urging on his oxen: "Gee, gee, gee up!" The oxen barely moved and the wheels screeched stridently, setting up a racket that grated on one's ears. This didn't seem to please the rooster either, for at each turn of the ponderous wheels it would claw

Benjamin with its trussed feet and crow with all its might. Benjamin lay prostrate as if in a daze, with all his limbs benumbed. Just think of what he'd been through: fright, hunger, rain and cold! He imagined that he had been captured in some desert by a Bedouin and was now being carried off into slavery.

"If he would sell me to a Jew, at least," the wretched Benjamin mused, "there may be some chance of deliverance. But what if he sells me to some Pasha or, God forbid, to some Pasha's daughter? In that case I'm lost — lost forever!" And at that very point the story of Joseph and Zuleika, Potiphar's wife, flashed through his head, and in his misery he heaved a profound sigh. The muzhik, hearing him sigh, turned round:

"Well, are you feeling a trifle better, little Jew?"

Benjamin's head had cleared a little by now and things were gradually coming back to him. However, he found himself in a new predicament: he understood hardly any Russian. What was he to do, then? How could he communicate with the Gentile in order to find out where he was taking him? He made an effort to sit up but failed: his legs and feet were full of shooting pains.

"Are you feeling a trifle better?" the muzhik repeated his question, ending with his "Gee, gee, gee up!"

"Yes — better. But my — " Benjamin pointed to his feet, not knowing what they were called in Russian — "*ai, ai, ai!*"

"Where are you from, little Jew? Gee, gee, gee up!"

"Where is this Jew from?" Benjamin echoed the other in singsong. "Why, I'm Niumka-Biniumka from Tuneyadevka —"

"You're from Tuneyadevka? But tell me, why are you staring at me as if you were daft? Or maybe you really are daft — may the devil take your mother! Gee, gee, gee up!"

"I . . . why, I just told you — I'm none other than Niumka from Tuneyadevka," said Benjamin, struggling in a hodgepodge of Russian, Hebrew and Yiddish, making a piteous grimace and gesturing imploringly. "May it please you . . . in Tuneyadevka . . . my wife will give you . . . a little vodka and a Sabbath loaf, and thank you for your kindness — "

The muzhik evidently grasped the meaning of Benjamin's farrago.

"That's good, little Jew!" said he and, turning round, began to urge on his oxen again, while Benjamin crawled back under the overcoat.

Several hours later the cart rumbled into the Tuneyadevka market place. Men and women quickly gathered round the cart.

"How much for that rooster? How much for your onions?" some voice was shouting.

"You got eggs, maybe? Or potatoes?" another vociferated.

But at this point one of the men broke in with: "Say, friend, did you happen to see a Jew on the road, maybe? One Biniumka — he's missing, vanished just as if the river had swallowed him up!"

Before the bewildered muzhik could make any reply, the women had clustered about the cart like locusts, thrown back the coarse cloth coat, and screamed as if with one voice: "Benjamin!"

"He's here! Tzipeh-Kroine! Bassheva-Braindel! Run quick with the good news to Zelda — that which she has lost has been found! She isn't a wretched deserted wife any more!"

All was in tumult from then on; Tuneyadevka was in an uproar; young and old came running from all over to have a peep at Benjamin. They showered him with all sorts of questions, and retold their adventures in hunting for him high and low during the preceding day and night, and how they had already given him up for a martyr to Israel and looked on his Zelda as a poor *agunah.* *

Zelda came running up in the midst of all this hubbub, wringing her hands and weeping at the sight of her husband, pale as death and woebegone. She wavered for a moment between giving her bedraggled mate a tongue-lashing and pouring out all the bitterness in her heart upon him, or rejoicing at God's great mercy in saving her from the sinister status of deserted wife.

Within a matter of minutes Benjamin, sprawled out on a sack of potatoes and followed by a great procession, rolled homeward on the cart through the market place. The townfolk of Tuneyadevka, young and old, needed no prodding to pay their respects to him, and escorted him with spontaneous outcries of "Martyr! Martyr! Martyr!" "Martyr" was to stick to him throughout his life. He became known as Benjamin the Martyr, and his wife as Zelda the Deserted.

* According to Jewish law, a woman who, her husband having disappeared (for whatever reason), is without a bill of divorcement and cannot remarry.

That same day Tuneyadevka's home-grown medico came to Benjamin and administered all the remedies in his pharmacopeia: he applied leeches, cupped him, shaved his head bald as an egg, and suggested that it behooved Benjamin, if, with God's help, he felt strong enough, to go to the synagogue, no later than the next morning, and offer up the Benediction for Deliverance from Peril.

BENJAMIN'S FRUSTRATED attempts, the misadventure that
had caused so much misery to his wife and given rise to
so much gossip on the market place, in the synagogue,
and in the bathhouse, should have, one might have
thought, served to knock out of his head any notion of
traveling into far-off lands — on the contrary, it made
him more resolved than ever. Thereafter he regarded
himself with the assurance and respect due a hardened
adventurer who had gone through adversity and had
been put to crucial tests, and yet had triumphed over all
vicissitudes. He fancied himself a giant and a sage, well
versed in the Seven Wisdoms which were to be found
only in *The Image of the World,* who had read widely
and was familiar with what went on in the world. He
took to self-pity on finding himself, to use a literary
phrase, "like a rose amid thorns," and in Tuneyadevka,
at that, of all places, where the dull-witted townsmen
couldn't see an inch beyond their noses. Instead of
dampening his spirit, however, the jeering sallies he was
undergoing just then impelled him still more to undertake the travels he had in mind.

"If the Lord would but grant me (he mused) to make
my pilgrimage to distant climes, and return in peace with
happy tidings and consolation for our brethren, after

being honored the world over! Every mother's son in Tuneyadevka would then learn who I, Benjamin, really am!"

Benjamin's projected journey had meanwhile been delayed by a few minor difficulties. First of all, where was he to get the necessary funds? He never had as much as a copper in his pocket. He spent all his time in the synagogue, and it was his wife who provided for the household, running a small shop that she had set up shortly after the expiration of *kest.** Not that her entire stock in trade amounted to much; if, in addition to the shop, she hadn't also managed to knit stockings, pluck feathers during the evening, and accumulate rendered chicken fat for resale on the eve of Passover, to say nothing of driving a good bargain at the fair, now and then, they wouldn't have been able to keep body and soul together. Could he sell some household belongings, perhaps? But what did he have to sell? The two candlesticks that Zelda had inherited from her great-grandparents, over which candlesticks she said the Benediction of the Lights on the eve of Sabbath and which she treasured so? As to jewelry, she had none to speak of, unless it was an old silver ring set with a single pearl and which was kept under lock and key, except when she had to attend some great occasion. Or should he offer for sale his shabby Sabbath gabardine, dating back to his wedding day and now out at the elbows and so threadbare that the faded lining showed here and there? And, sure

* The custom, among the Jews of Eastern Europe, of the wife's parents supporting the married couple for a certain period.

enough, he had an overcoat as well — if one could call it that. At the time of Benjamin's marriage his father — may his memory be blessed! — had ordered a coat for him, pledging himself to line it with sheepskin and to put a collar of squirrel fur on it, whenever the balance of the dowry came through. But, the dowry never having got beyond the verbal stage, the garment had done duty for many years even in its half-finished state.

Benjamin's other problem was, how was he to leave home? Should he talk the matter over with his spouse, should he divulge his grandiose scheme to her? God forbid! Pandemonium would break loose; there would be no end to her wailing and moaning and, to top it all off, she would think him a madman. For how could you expect a simple housewife to fathom such abstruse matters. A housewife, be she even as full of virtues as a biblical matron, still remained nothing more than a simple housewife. Should he leave home secretly, without so much as a goodbye? That didn't seem right; that smacked too much of the sort of thing that the Litvacks [Lithuanian Jews] did. On the other hand, to abandon his plan, to give up the voyage, was out of the question. That would be tantamount to suicide. For travel had by now become second nature to Benjamin. Every Jew must pray three times a day, but Benjamin was by now thinking of his journey at every moment of the day, and even dreamt of it at night. So much under the sway was he of his ruling passion, so conditioned and attuned to the impending voyage had his senses of hearing and sight become, that he seemed oblivious to the immediate scene and envisioned only the wonders of the Promised Land. When someone spoke to him he was likely as not to come up with such irrelevant things as: *India, Sambatyon, Antikuda, Great Viper, Lindenworm, ass, carob pod, Turk, Tartar, brigand,* along with a jumble of other such words.

He had to set out on his journey; of that there was no question. But how was he to surmount the obstacles looming ahead? If there were but a single person to whom he could have turned!

One man of that sort there was in Tuneyadevka, however: Senderel, named after his great-grandfather, Reb Senderel. This Senderel was a simple-minded, unassuming man, without any tricks or guile in him. In the House of Prayer his place was behind the reader's platform, in itself an indication that he was not of the town's elite. He listened in silence to the discourses and disputations in the House of Prayer, as though he were a stranger. And when on some rare occasion he did make a comment, no matter how serious in intent, it merely provoked merriment and jibes on the part of those present, so far was it from conveying anything profound or novel. He was no more than a butt for the town wags, but was never resentful when people snickered, inasmuch as he was a kindly sort of man by nature, something like a placid, docile cow. He didn't know what it was to take issue with anybody. If someone laughed — well, let him: the fellow laughing undoubtedly enjoyed it. It must be admitted, however, that once in a while an utterance of Senderel's, without himself being aware of it, did harbor a really sound idea.

People loved to play pranks on him, so that on Tishah

37

be-Av* there were far more burrs entangled in his beard and sidelocks than in anybody else's, while on Hoshana Rabba,† when pranksters pelt one another with cushions during the vigil, Senderel was bound to receive more than his share. On the other hand, he would come in for the least share of the hard buckwheat crackers and brandy distributed on the anniversary of someone's death.

Senderel was always the scapegoat and, unlike other people, the least stubborn of men. If someone preferred things a certain way, he readily agreed. Senderel went along with the wishes of others not out of any self-effacement but because it offered the easiest way. "What do I care?" he was in the habit of saying. "You want things just that way; so be it, then."

Among little boys Senderel was himself a boy. He liked to be with them and like them. Senderel, in their midst, was like some tame animal that lets the youngsters romp and frisk about it and ride upon its back, and the urchins did just that, tugging at his beard into the bargain. When passers-by chided the small fry: "Have some respect for an elder person, a man with a beard, you good-for-nothings! Why do you pull his beard?" — "No matter, no matter!" Senderel would rally to the youngsters' defense. "What do I care? Let them have a little fun!"

It wasn't all milk and honey for him at home, either; his wife was the breadwinner and man of the family. She

---

* The ninth of Av, a fast day in commemoration of the destruction of the Temple.
† Hoshana Rabba, the seventh day of the Feast of Tabernacles.

kept him under her thumb and even kicked and cuffed him on occasion, and he had had to resign himself to his unenviable lot. With the coming of the holidays she would tie a kerchief over his matted beard and make him whitewash the walls and give the house a thorough cleaning. He also had to peel the potatoes and make the noodles, clean and stuff the fish, carry the firewood and start the stove, just like any housewife — and the folks had in fact nicknamed him *die Yiddine,* "Senderel the Housewife." And it was this Senderel the Housewife whom our Benjamin has chosen as confidant. Why Senderel, of all people, you ask? Because Benjamin, for some reason or other, had always felt drawn toward him. They had much in common and frequently saw things eye to eye, so that Benjamin always found it a pleasure to talk to him. It's quite possible, too, that Benjamin took into consideration Senderel's lack of resistance; Senderel would be bound to agree to his plan and submit to all his wishes. And even if Senderel were to take exception to a point or two, Benjamin felt that with his eloquence he would be able to win the other over.

When Benjamin came to Senderel he found him sitting on the dairy bench, peeling potatoes. One cheek looked inflamed, while one of his eyes was black and blue. He sat there dejected and crestfallen, like a woman who had just received a drubbing at her husband's hands. Senderel's wife wasn't home.

"Good morning, Senderel! Why so blue?" Benjamin accosted him. "Eh? Has she been at you again? Where is that woman?"

"She's out marketing."

"Fine!" Benjamin was overjoyed. "Stop peeling those potatoes, my friend, and come with me into the next room. I don't want anybody meddling with us now; I want to have a heart-to-heart talk with you. I have no more patience. Hurry up, or she'll come home and raise a fuss before I've told you everything."

"What do I care — if you're in a hurry, let's hurry," Senderel remarked, and followed him into the next room.

"Tell me something, Senderel," Benjamin began. "Do you know what lies beyond Tuneyadevka?"

"Yes, beyond Tuneyadevka there's Prichepe [Pick-a-Fight], where you can get a good glass vodka now and then — "

"You're a born fool, Senderel! I mean farther on, much farther than that!"

"Farther than even Prichepe?" Senderel was astonished. "No, I don't know of any place beyond that. And you, Benjamin — do you know?"

"Do I know! You ask whether I know! There's a whole world of wonders for you lying farther on, I tell you!" Benjamin said, beside himself with rapture, as if he were another Columbus and had just discovered America.

"What, for instance?"

"There's" — Benjamin swelled with emotion — "there's the Great Viper, there's the Lindenworm."

"You mean the shamir with which King Solomon hewed the stones for the Holy Temple?" asked the wide-eyed Senderel.

"Yes, my friend. Yes — in the Land of Israel, ever so far away! Would you like to visit it? Eh?"

"And what about you?"

"What a question! I do want to, Senderel — and I'll be there before long."

"I envy you, Benjamin. There, I think, you'll eat carob pods and dates to your heart's content."

"You too can eat them, Senderel. You have as much right to be in the Land of Israel as I."

"That I have. But how does one get there? That's where the Turks live, they say."

"There's protection against them, Senderel. Tell me, do you know anything about the Red Jews?"

"I've heard all sorts of tales about them around the synagogue stove; but just where they live, and how one gets to them — that's something I don't know. If I knew, I wouldn't hold back on you. Why not tell you? What do I care?"

"Ha, ha! But I do know, you see!" Benjamin exclaimed with overweening pride, as he pulled *In Praise of Jerusalem* out of his pocket. "Listen to what it says here — I'll read it to you: 'When I arrived in Bruti' — so it is written here — 'I came upon four Jews from Babylon. I conversed with one of them, named Rabbi Moshe and well versed in Hebrew, who told me some authentic stories about the River Sambatyon.* He had heard them from certain Ishmaelites who had beheld this river, and he had also been told that the *Bene Moshe,* the Ten Lost Tribes of Israel, are living thereabouts.' Further on he

---

* A legendary river, in constant agitation during weekdays, flinging stones high into the air, but completely at rest on the Sabbath.

says (and I quote his exact words): 'A certain rich man informed me that some thirty years ago a wanderer, reputedly of the Tribe of Simeon, had visited him, and had likewise reported that the region beyond was inhabited by four tribes, one of which, the Tribe of Issachar, devotes all its time to the study of the Torah, and that one of this tribe is king over all four tribes.'

"In addition to that, it is also written in the *Travels of Benjamin:* 'From there it is a journey of some twenty days to the mountains of Nisbon, on the banks of Lake Gozan. Four of the tribes, namely: Dan, Zebulun, Asher and Naphtali dwell in the Nisbon Mountains. They have provinces and cities. Lake Gozan cuts them off from the rest of the land. They are governed by a king named Rabbi Joseph Amarkla ha-Levi, and are free from the rule of any other potentate. They have an alliance with the infidel Turks.' There are, besides, ever so many more things recorded about the Rechabites in the land of Tema who are governed by a Jewish sovereign and observe fast days and recite special prayers for the Jews scattered in exile. Now, what do you think, my friend, what if they were suddenly to behold me, their brother Benjamin from Tuneyadevka, come to see them? Do tell me, Senderel — what do you think of that?"

"How could they help but rejoice to see you, Benjamin? A most welcome guest; every one of them, perhaps even King Amarkla himself would invite you to a feast. Well, anyway, remember me to them. If it were at all possible I'd gladly go along with you."

"Ha!" Benjamin uttered in surprise, as a new idea

popped into his head. "Ha! Perhaps you really should come along with me, Senderel? Here's your chance, the chance of a lifetime, foolish one. I intend to go there anyway — and two would be company. And if by some stroke of luck I should become king, I'd make you my right-hand man. Shake hands on it! Why should you stagnate here, foolish one, and suffer hell on earth at the hands of your shrew of a wife? See what that spitfire of yours did to your cheek! Come along, Senderel. God willing, you won't regret it."

"Well, if you wish things that way," Senderel said, falling in with the plan, "so be it! As to *her* — I won't take being away from her too much to heart. I'd be a block-head to tell her what I'm about!"

"You're all right! Let me hug you!" Benjamin went into raptures. "You've taken a load off my shoulders; you've solved a problem that had me baffled. I'll put it in your own words: As to *her* — *my* wife, I mean — I won't take being away from her too much to heart, either. But there's still another difficulty: where are we to get money for the road?"

"Money? What money? You don't expect to buy a new wardrobe, or even to patch up your gabardine for the road, do you? If you ask me, old clothes are best for traveling. And we'll most certainly get new gabardines when we get to where we're going."

"That's true enough. No need to worry about that. But we do need a little cash — for food, say — on our long journey."

"What sort of food are you talking about, Benjamin?

You're not expecting to carry along a field kitchen, by any chance, are you? Is there any lack of inns and houses on the road?"

"Explain yourself, Senderel. I don't understand what you're driving at," said Benjamin, looking puzzled.

"As long as there are houses on the road, we can beg from door to door. What do all the other Jews do? Some go begging today, and others will beg on the morrow. It's an ancient Jewish custom: merely a free loan — "

"You're right again, as true as I'm alive!" Benjamin saw the light. "In that case, the Lord be thanked, we're provided with everything and are prepared for the journey. We can start out right at daybreak, when everybody is still asleep. It's a sin, however, to waste time now. What do you say?"

"If you want things that way, so be it!"

"In that case I'll steal out of the house tomorrow morning, Senderel. I'll be waiting for you near the deserted windmill. Remember, now — tomorrow morning, and be there early! Remember!" said Benjamin with emphasis, and started toward the door.

"Just a moment, Benjamin! Benjamin, just a moment!" Senderel began rummaging in the bosom of his shirt and at last got out a torn, soiled handkerchief, with ever so many knots. "You see this little hoard, Benjamin? These are my savings — the little cash I managed to salt away right under my wife's nose, ever since our wedding day. It'll come in handy at the beginning, eh?"

"I could kiss you, so I could!" and Benjamin, overwhelmed, embraced Senderel.

"Look at the love birds!" a shrill voice took the pair by surprise at this point. "Look at them, will you — when the goat's got into the house and is devouring all the potatoes! May the worms eat your flesh!"

It was Senderel's wife who had so suddenly appeared on the scene and was now cursing them. She stood there, firmly rooted, her eyes ablaze with wrath, one hand pointing at the goat, the other beckoning her husband to her. Resigned to his fate, and like a guilty urchin expecting a whipping, Senderel slowly approached his tormentor.

"Courage, my friend! You're hearing that shrew's song for the last time! Remember — tomorrow!" whispered Benjamin, and tiptoed out.

NEXT MORNING, long before the cowherds had driven their cattle to pasture, our Benjamin, hugging a bundle, was standing impatiently near the windmill. That bundle contained all the items he deemed essential for such a journey, to wit: prayer shawl and phylacteries, the prayer book *Path of Life,* the book *A Statute for Israel,* the Psalms and several books without which, like a craftsman deprived of his tools, he would have been helpless. His Sabbath gabardine was also tucked in the bundle: one must make an appearance before the world. And, in addition to that, he had a few coppers which he had filched from under his wife's pillow. In short, he was, praised be the Lord, well equipped and fitted out for his travels.

Meanwhile the glowing sun gradually came up on the horizon, brightening the entire countryside. Its radiance had an exhilarating effect on all things. The trees and the grass welcomed it, smiling through their tears of dew, like children bursting into laughter through their tears when shown a gaudy plaything. Birds were wheeling and chirping around Benjamin, as though in salutation: "Come, let us cheer and sing a paean of triumph to the great personage standing near the windmill — let us sing to Benjamin of Tuneyadevka, the Alexander of Macedon of his time, who is bidding farewell to the place of his birth and who is leaving his wife and children behind him, to embark on a holy mission, going wherever his eyes may lead him! There he stands, the great Benjamin who, like the sun, has left his night's shelter, anxious to set foot on the path of adventure! With the prowess of a leopard and the swiftness of an eagle he is prepared to do the will of our Father in Heaven! Warble and trill, break into song, so that his heart may be gladdened and rejoice!"

And Benjamin felt truly elated.

"Am I not the most fortunate man in the world?" he mused. "What do I lack — may I be spared the Evil Eye! My wife — praised be His Name! — I have provided for; she can find bread in her little shop. I myself am as free as the fowl of the air. The entire world lies open before me; with my skill and natural endowments, with my grasp of the Seven Wisdoms, no man such as I can perish. Besides, I am a Jew who is not wholly without faith. And, all else aside, God does not forsake those Jews who have faith."

Benjamin's inner ecstasy manifested itself in song. He hummed a hymn of praise to the All-Highest which blended with the chirping of the birds and crickets and the buzzing of the flies and ascended to the Throne of Glory in the Seventh Heaven.

Meanwhile time passed and there was as yet no sign of Senderel. This irked and worried Benjamin. He scanned the horizon, he looked intently in every direction, but all in vain.

Could that virago, Senderel's wife, have delegated

some housework to him at the last moment? But that seemed hardly likely — the town was still fast asleep. The peeling of potatoes would come much later; that task was undertaken by the housewives only after the customary round of bickering with their husbands, spanking the children, and hanging out the bedclothes to air.

Benjamin, on tenterhooks, was at a loss as to what to do. Should he return home? But that was unthinkable. Alexander of Macedon had burned the bridges over which he had crossed to India, so that he would not be able to turn back. On the other hand, to go without Senderel was just as much out of the question. Senderel was indispensable to him; to set out without him now would be like navigating the high seas in a schooner without a rudder, or administering a kingdom without a premier.

Suddenly Benjamin made out in the distance a fellow creature bearing all the earmarks of Senderel who yet wasn't Senderel; this creature had on a skirt made of calico and woman's headgear. Benjamin's heart sank and he turned white as a ghost: was this his wife, perhaps, all ablaze with wrath, come to pour out all the bitterness in her heart and to drag him back into bondage?

"God only knows," these are Benjamin's own words, "what I endured at that painful moment. I would rather have welcomed a hundred vipers than my spouse. For a viper stings the body only, whereas an angry wife stings one to the very soul. But the Almighty lent me strength and I ran for cover behind the windmill, watching keenly as an eagle from my vantage point."

As the figure became clearly discernible, Benjamin leaped forward, frantic with joy, bellowing: "Hey, Senderel!"

Senderel was wearing a calico duster, with his face bandaged in a soiled kerchief and both his eyes blackened; he had a cane in his hand and a great pack slung across his shoulders, but he seemed as fair in Benjamin's sight as a bride arrayed for the wedding seems in the eyes of her groom.

"Even as the hart panteth after the water of the brook," writes Benjamin, "as the desert-parched traveler rejoiceth when he cometh upon the fresh waters of a mountain stream, so did I pant after and rejoice over Senderel, my tried and true companion."

"What happened, Senderel? Why did you keep me waiting here so long?"

"Well, I had to go to your house first," said Senderel in excuse. "By the time I got there and woke up your wife Zelda, quite some time had gone by."

"You woke up Zelda?" Benjamin screamed, staggered by the new complication. "What made you do that, you imbecile?"

"What made me do that?" Senderel became confused. "After knocking on the woodshed door and getting no answer, I started banging away on the house door: *Knock, knock, knock!* So when Zelda, scared out of her wits, stuck out her head, I asked for you."

"Senderel, we're sunk! You've certainly made a mess of things. Zelda is sure to follow us and — "

"Don't let that worry you, Benjamin. Zelda flew into a rage and screamed: 'You can go to all the black devils,

49

together with my dear husband!' and slammed the door in my face. I sort of lost my bearings for a moment, but after a while I remembered our appointment at the windmill and it dawned on me that when she started cursing she must have had an inkling of where you were."

"What's that? What did you say, Senderel? She saw me? Maybe she's after us right now?"

"God forbid, Benjamin! No sooner did she slam the door than I shouted at her: 'Is there anything you want me to tell your husband, Zelda? Or do you want to send him something, maybe?' — but there wasn't another sound out of her. She must be one of those sound sleepers. So, as a parting shot, I said: 'You've gone back to sleep, Zelda? Sleep well, then.' That's what I said, and went off."

These last words seemed to bring Benjamin back to life. He breathed more freely; his troubled mind had been relieved of a great weight. A new sparkle came into his eyes.

"Now, Senderel!" he cried out in great spirits. "Now — start off with the right foot!"

From a swamp nearby the croaking of frogs rose up as if bidding farewell to the two world travelers. And the croaking of Tuneyadevka frogs has a most uncommon sound, as celebrated as the nimbleness of the cockroaches of Dnieprovitz.

OUR WAYFARERS started out at a brisk pace, as though they had torn loose from their moorings, or were being driven along by whiplashes. Their unbuttoned gabardines flapping in the wind reminded one of two-masted schooners with bellying sails scudding over a watery expanse. Upon my word, some of our local stagecoach drivers would wish for no greater speed on the part of their teams. Crows and ravens swaggering over the highway were daunted by the two quaint, nimble-footed scarecrows and took to flight, cawing loudly.

The enthusiasm and happiness of the two at that moment baffle all description. They were happy as clams at high tide and could have embraced the whole world. Senderel seemed jubilant, having, at last, escaped his shrew of a wife. The preceding day was particularly associated in his mind with evil fortune, with black-and-blue bruises and a plucked beard. May you, you other henpecked husbands, be spared such cordial morning greetings as Senderel had got from his wife!

The two kept up their rapid pace without uttering a word. By now they were drenched with sweat. Senderel, footsore, exhausted, and gasping like a fish out of water, stopped to catch his breath.

"Faster, faster, Senderel!" Benjamin encouraged him, accelerating his own pace and marching like some warrior of old.

"Have a heart, Benjamin! I can't keep up with you. You're as swift as the roe on the mountains, you skip like a billy goat before the flock!"

"Hurry, Senderel! I could run along like this to the ends of the earth!" Benjamin called out again.

"But what's all that rush, Benjamin? Tell me, I beg of you," pleaded Senderel. "We won't miss anything, believe me. What if we do get to where we're going a day, or even several days, later? The world isn't coming to an end yet — the way I've heard it, it's destined to last to the year seven thousand, and that's a good many hundred years yet."

"Faster, Senderel! We can't afford to waste any time. The sooner we get away from here the better. Have a little more patience, and when we get to journey's end you'll rest your weary bones and live like a prince."

"Indeed, you're right, Benjamin. You want me to step along a little faster — faster let it be. What do I care? But those feet of mine — what can you do about them?"

Benjamin had to slow down a bit for the sake of his friend; there was no help for it.

When the Lord had drawn the sun from its sheath, its luminous rays sent down such heat that the travelers had to drop down in exhaustion near a wayside thicket, and lay there sweating profusely and gasping. Yesterday's scratches on Senderel's face, stung by the dripping sweat, felt as though they were being pricked with needles.

After a short breathing spell their first concern was to don prayer shawls and phylacteries and chant the morning prayers. Benjamin worshiped fervently, out of the fulness of his heart, swaying to and fro. Such devotions deserved a good drink — but where was he to get it? And if he could but have a bite of something to eat! After such a forced march he was famished and could have devoured a mountain of food, yet he hadn't a piece of bread the size of an olive. He looked this way and that, cracked his knuckles, yawned, scratched himself, smacked his lips, stroked his beard and sidelocks and, finally, got out a tiny book, proceeding to drone the words to the melody of *Akdamut.**

"Senderel, can you guess why I've turned to these prayers?" Benjamin asked during a moment's pause.

"You must be hungry," Senderel conjectured.

"And what if I am?"

"That's why you're chanting, Benjamin," Senderel remarked. "There's a saying that a Jew chants to forget his hunger pangs."

"You don't quite grasp it; I'll explain things to you," Benjamin temporized.

Senderel, however, plunged his hand into his pack and drew out a small bag. When Benjamin glimpsed its contents a delectable warmth spread through his limbs. That bag was full of all good things: rye bread, the ends of a white loaf left over from the Sabbath, salt, cucumbers, radishes, onions and garlic! Senderel, like a capable housewife, had remembered to make proper provision for the journey and had taken all these essentials along. His prestige mounted considerably in Benjamin's eyes.

* *Akdamut,* Aramaic hymn sung at the Feast of Weeks.

"It is God Who has sent me this Senderel," Benjamin reflected, "even as He sent manna to the children of Israel in the desert!"

After the repast Senderel stored away whatever was left.

"We'll need these things once more — and the sack a thousand times over, for the rest of our lives, maybe. It'll come in handy when we go begging from door to door. God — praised be His Name — will stand by us," he soliloquized.

The place of the fairy-tale tablecloth, which produces food when commanded: "Tablecloth, tablecloth, provide us with food!" is, among us Jews, taken by the sack. A multitude of souls thrive by means of this very sack, and it is bequeathed as a legacy even unto the second and third generations. The sack is substantially the same throughout the length and breadth of the land, but in so motley a throng it naturally assumes various forms. Among the common folk it is the traditional plain sack of homespun; in the upper strata, however, in the fashionable world, it passes under such guises as a sine-cure in a small congregation, an alms box, a free-loan society on a modest scale, and suchlike manifestations; essentially, however, it is still the same immemorial beggar's sack.

"Senderel," Benjamin warmed up, evidently impressed by the other's comment, "Senderel, we two are a pair from heaven, you might say, like body and soul. While you concern yourself with corporeal matters, such as provender for our journey, I look after things spiritual.

Incidentally, do you know why I am reciting the *Akdamut* hymn? There's a deep purpose behind that. When the Lord — praised be His Name — shall have brought us safe and sound to the *Bene Moshe*, I say to myself, we ought to be able to converse with them. It is said that they speak a language that is partly Targum, but mostly they talk in the *Akdamut* language. Eldad ha-Dani, who came to us from that region, had, I think, a hand in writing the *Akdamut* hymn. Bear in mind then, Senderel, that though in our parts one can get by with our pudding-German, over there they probably won't understand German."

"In that sort of thing I depend entirely upon you," Senderel assured him with proper deference. "You're a learned man, Benjamin, you delve in the holy writings, and you undoubtedly know what you're doing and where you're heading. Just to show you how much I trust you — I hadn't asked you if we're on the right track. You're on the go — and that's all I care about. Go on and I'll follow, even as a calf follows its dam."

Benjamin felt deeply honored by Senderel's implicit trust. He saw himself as a captain steering his ship through turbulent seas. Just the same, the praise had not blinded him to the stark reality of his having no idea of where they were and the possibility that they might have gone astray. While he was pondering this, a loaded hay-cart, driven by a peasant, came lumbering toward them.

"I say, Senderel," Benjamin suggested, "it wouldn't do any harm to ask that Gentile for directions. Go and ask him, just for curiosity's sake. In this strange hinterland you'd do better to talk to the peasant in his own coarse speech, for you've accompanied your wife to the fairs often enough."

Senderel advanced a few paces toward the peasant, meekly enough, and blurted out:

"Good day to you! Tell me, my dear man — which is the road to Eretz Israel, the Land of Israel?"

"What's that?" said the peasant, seeming irked. "Which Israel? What Israel am I supposed to have seen?" and he halted his horses.

"No, no!" Benjamin broke in, still keeping at a distance. "Senderel, tell him more distinctly — he's got only a peasant's head on his shoulders."

"To *Eretz Israel* — which way?" Senderel repeated more clearly.

"The devil alone can figure you Jews out! What are you bothering my head for? This is the road to Pievki [Leechville], and here you are pestering me for directions to some 'Eretzisrael' or other!" said the peasant, mimicking Senderel, spat, and drove on.

Our wayfarers plodded on again. Benjamin had stinging pains in his calves, and his feet — may you be spared anything of the kind — felt as though they were amputated, yet he spurred himself on and kept walking. Since he found it hard to keep up his former stride, he resorted to a sort of hop-skip-and-jump. Of course, his pace had diminished somewhat, yet walk on he did. For at this point he had to face the grim facts. What else was he to do? Lie down in the road? — may that befall only the enemies of Zion! What purpose would that serve? Besides, how could a Jew collapse on the highway, without any rhyme or reason? It would merely distress Senderel and, God forbid, retard their progress. In short, they kept on walking all day long. And by nightfall, with the help of God, they reached Pievki without any mishap.

The pair had barely set foot in the inn when Benjamin slumped down in a corner to rest his weary limbs. Senderel, however, like the good housewife he was, proceeded to forage for food. The innkeeper took in Senderel and his garb from head to foot, and realized that the guest confronting him was not of the common run of those who crossed his threshold. After greeting him amiably, the innkeeper asked him his name and where he came from. Senderel was his name, the guest let it be known, one who had a little bit of a claim to being a Jew of the Holy Land; he was a follower of Reb Benjamin, now reposing in that corner over there.

Assuming an air of piety, the innkeeper paused for a moment and invited the wanderer to take a seat.

Let the Princess (that is, Senderel) carry on his small talk with the innkeeper, then, while we turn our attention to the Prince (that is, Benjamin).

When our Benjamin, all worn out, had slumped down in his corner, he was virtually oblivious to the outside world. The veins on his legs were swollen and his feet burned as if biting ants were burrowing under the skin. His ears throbbed with an unbearable din and his head hummed from a charivari of exploding fireworks and spluttering rockets that burst into myriad colors, only to be swallowed up in total blackness.

In his half-comatose state Benjamin suddenly thought he had heard the jingling of distant bells, coming nearer and growing louder, and finally the screech of wagon wheels halting in front of the gate. This was followed by a hubbub of shrill and hoarse voices, as though the whole town had gathered for some important matter. When cats are scampering on a roof, we know why they've come together there, even though we are ignorant of what their caterwauling means. But, it was next to impossible to determine what all this cacophony of catcalls, laughter, shouts and cheers was about. Whoever could get to the bottom of all this? And before Benjamin knew it, the door flew open and a great throng tumbled into the house.

He tried to withdraw still deeper into his corner. By now a great many candles, such as are used on the Sabbath, lighted up the room as bright as day. Some of the candlesticks were clogged with old wicks and the candles were all but falling out, while in others the candles were propped up somehow or other. Wandering musicians were tuning their instruments at one side of the square oaken table; each string responded to the touch of the fiddler, as if communing with its master; the flute player and the cymbalist were also getting ready; only the blind drummer, his thick mane falling over his eyes, was napping in a corner. A queer fellow, standing on a stool, was performing for the crowd, eliciting peals of laughter at his every sally.

"In honor of the parents of the bridal pair, in honor of the master of the house and of the welcome guests, strike up a tune!"

The musicians struck up, and everybody joined in a sort of round dance, revolving counterclockwise.

And it was at this point that one of the dancers tripped over Benjamin and raised a hullabaloo: "Well, if it isn't our long-lost Benjamin, our treasure! There he is!"

Among those crowding round him Benjamin recognized certain of his friends, as well as the rabbi from Tuneyadevka.

"Come, Benjamin, join us in the dance!" he heard them urge him.

"Believe me, I can hardly stand up!" he pleaded.

"Don't let that worry you!" someone insisted. "Come along — you'll survive! Come on, now — we're going to tell on you, anyway!"

"Don't say anything to Zelda, whatever you do!" said Benjamin, quite alarmed.

"Come on, then!" they teased him.

"Have mercy, fellow Jews! Please believe me — I can't do it! There's something I can tell only to the rabbi."

By now Benjamin was the center of attraction. But, as he drew the rabbi close to him in order to whisper his deep secret in the other's very ear, he was surprised by a terrific blow.

The pain awoke him from his deep sleep; he rubbed his eyes and saw, in the wan moonlight falling into his dark corner, that he was hugging a calf.

What was going on? How had a calf come to be here? Could it be that he, Benjamin, had calved? Let us assume that he was, in many ways, a cow, but, even so, he was but a two-legged one — and who had ever heard of a two-legged cow calving? True, we do have a good many calves, and that among our best people, but they are, after all, calves in human guise. And some of them — the heifers — are actually attractive, with lovely features, whereas this calf was nothing of the sort. How did it ever get here? It must have dropped down from the skies!

No, my friends, don't ever believe in heavenly calves. The whole thing can be explained rather simply.

When Benjamin, more dead than alive, had dropped down in his corner, he had failed to notice the calf beside him. During his nightmare it was the innkeeper's calf instead of the Tuneyadevka rabbi he had embraced as he whispered the secret of the travels he was undertaking. And since the calf had no fondness for Benjamin's embrace, it had kicked him.

When Benjamin was fully awake, he let go the animal and tried to get out of his fix. The calf likewise tried to free itself, and in the process butted Benjamin, at the same time noisily turning over a large tub of water and drenching our adventurer.

Senderel and the innkeeper, thoroughly alarmed and carrying candles, rushed in on the ludicrous scene. Had a poet been around he might have turned out a ballad, beginning:

> Neither in a pleasant nook,
> Or by a gloomy, marshy brook,
> Can love be thwarted
> Or true lovers parted.

THE COLD SHOWER and a night's rest had quite refreshed Benjamin. He perceived something of the miraculous in the incident with the calf — for hadn't his pains eased during the night? He tried to prove to Senderel that sinful man is wrong in complaining of an affliction; ill-fortune could lead to good: an ass could become the Lord's messenger; a gnat could unbearably torment (witness the one that had flown into the nose of Titus the Tyrant and had knocked against his brain with its brazen beak) — so why couldn't a calf work a cure as well as any doctor? Yesterday's incident served as a good omen that his journey was destined to succeed and that he would reach his goal without mishap.

"A water carrier passing by with full pails has been a good omen since time immemorial; how much more lucky, then, such a brimming vat as last night's!"

However, since the pains in his feet still persisted, and in part because of the comfort of his straw pallet as well, Benjamin tarried in Pievki for the rest of that day. He might have been compared to a ship stranded on a sand bar, and biding for wind and tide to set it afloat again.

Next day the pair resumed their journey. Benjamin was plodding along grimly, without uttering a word, when suddenly he stopped in his tracks: "Eh, Senderel," said he mournfully, "there's something I forgot — "

"What was it?" Senderel said, growing anxious, at the same time reaching for his pack.

"I forgot it at home, Senderel — there's something I forgot at home."

"You're imagining things, Benjamin!" said Senderel, trying to soothe him. "We packed everything needed for a long journey: the sack, thank God, is here; here are a prayer shawl and the phylacteries, our prayer books and Sabbath gabardine — we've got everything, in short. What else do we need — what could we have left out?"

"The thing I forgot, Senderel, is extremely important — a matter of life and death, you might say. I do hope everything will go well. The only thing is, if something untoward should happen to us on the road, God forbid, we shall realize the grave importance of what I've forgotten to do. We were in such a hurry to leave that I forgot to recite a certain incantation, recorded in an ancient holy book. This incantation must be chanted at the city barrier when one starts out on a journey, and it is said that it will prove a safeguard against any evil dispensation. That's what I forgot, Senderel!"

"Are you thinking of turning back, by any chance?" Senderel asked.

"Have you gone out of your mind, or what?" Benjamin said, flushing in anger. "What do you mean by talking of turning back — after we've covered such a distance? What will the world think of you?"

"What do we care about the world?" Senderel interposed. "Did the world ask you to undertake the journey? Has it given you a written contract, along with your travel expenses?"

"Quite clever, indeed!" Benjamin mimicked him. "And

what about Alexander of Macedon — did the world ask him to go to India and wage war there? And all those travelers of our own nation — does the world ask them to wander from town to town?"

"For my part," Senderel commented, jovially, "they could all have stayed home. It would have worked out for the best of all concerned. What a fool this Alexander of Macedon was! He had everything his heart desired right at home; stay there and enjoy life! Why bother with India? And I'm even more baffled by the doings of our own brethren. Why don't they heed the wisdom of the proverb, and each cobbler stick to his last? People say a proverb, with all due allowance, is as good as a saying of the Talmud. What's the good of aimlessly wandering about, like vagabonds on a thorny path, draining the cup of bitterness, to say nothing of the waste of good shoe leather? As true as I'm a Jew, Benjamin, if I were to come on such a traveler, I'd remind him of this proverb!"

The pair kept disputing for some time, getting nowhere. Senderel might have been likened to a nag that generally does its master's bidding, yet now and then grows unruly and kicks over its traces. And while Benjamin did not actually whip the submissive Senderel, he did subdue him at last with a tongue-lashing. Senderel pricked up his ears, listened attentively to Benjamin's flow of language, and finally observed, after his wont: "You want things to be that way? So be it, then!"

And so Benjamin and the now tractable Senderel walked on over highways and byroads, until, all worn out, they entered the town of Teterevka.

Teterevka was the first sizable city that our wanderers

had ever seen. Little wonder, then, that they stared in admiration at the straight cobblestoned streets and gaped at the buildings, which seemed towering to them. They trod the sidewalks almost on tiptoe, as though afraid to profane the flagstones with their feet — countrified feet that do not fare so well in strange towns. Provincial feet that had known no flooring even in their homes, and that at the behest of their masters slogged through slush and mire — such feet turn wobbly, as though drunk, when they feel a stony surface beneath them, and become a little confused. Nor are such pedestrians hard to recognize.

Our Tuneyadevka adventurers walked humbly along, making way for everyone, Senderel occasionally pulling his friend aside. And once he himself got into a sort of grotesque dance with a gentleman who had come barging down the street and run into the stranger in the gabardine, who had instantly tried to move aside. No sooner did the gentleman step to the right, however, or to the left, than Senderel likewise veered in the same direction. This might have gone on indefinitely if the citizen, at last losing patience, had not unceremoniously grabbed Senderel by the collar and pushed him off the sidewalk into the mire of the gutter.

Everything in this city seemed strange and novel to our two travelers. They felt that they were being pointed at, the drivers shouted at them, glossy carriages were constantly rolling by, the buildings towered haughtily with their rows upon rows of glassily staring windows. Man and matter seemed to admonish them: "Show re-

spect, you beggars! Show respect, you country bump-
kins! Show respect!"

"You know what, Benjamin?" said Senderel, craning
his neck to view a tall structure. "I think we're in Stambul!"

"How can you say such a thing? Stambul, indeed!"
Benjamin said, snubbing him, as though he himself were
a native of that metropolis. "Stambul, I'll have you know,
has five hundred times five hundred streets, and each
street has five hundred times five hundred buildings,
each fifteen, twenty, or thirty stories high, and each one
accommodating five hundred times five hundred families. And do you think that is all? Not in the least! In
addition to these there are side streets, and market places,
and by-lanes, all as countless as the sands of the sea!"

"My, my, my!" said Senderel in awe. "That is really
awe-inspiring — there's a city for you! Do tell me, Benjamin — how have these great cities come about? To
think that people should all crowd into one place and
pile up one on top of another, as though the world had
become too small for them! There must be something to
this business of people straining to get away from the
earth and striving toward the heights — nearer to heaven.
Could it be, perhaps, that the human soul, conceived in
heaven, is drawn back toward it, ever higher — that it
yearns to spread its wings and soar to the very heights?
What do your philosophers have to say to that, Benjamin? Haven't you found some explanation for all this
in your books?"

"Philosophically speaking" — and here Benjamin knit

his brows — "there's quite a controversy raging on this point. As a matter of fact, I thrashed this matter out at one time around the stove in the House of Prayer, in connection with the passage in the Talmud: 'Ten portions of poverty were sent down upon earth — nine fell to Babylon, and one to the world as a whole,' as well as the passage in the Torah: 'And the earth was corrupt before God, and the earth was filled with violence.' But I will expound the matter for you. You've studied the Pentateuch, haven't you, Senderel? According to the Pentateuch, then, in the remote past our ancestors lived in tents, but during the Generation of Confusion all men gathered in one place and proceeded to bake bricks, for the building of a city whose structures would tower to the very skies. But before the building was really under way, the builders were seized by a mysterious confusion; one failed to understand the other, and the titanic scheme failed. Fortunately, the Almighty scattered them in time; the people cast off their trammels, began to breathe freely, and the world regained its sanity. But the iniquities of the Generation of Confusion have not as yet ceased altogether, and because of our many sins, because of man's lust for crowding, for swarming as the locusts do, for aspiring to the heights and reaching out for the skies, these iniquities still persist. 'And Abraham said to Lot: Let there be no strife, I pray thee, between me and thee; and between my herdmen and thy herdmen; for we are brethren. Is not the whole land before thee? Separate thyself, I pray thee, from me.' "

But before Benjamin could really get started on his scholarly discourse he and Senderel heard the gruff,

66

angry voice of a driver whose horses had nearly run them over.

"Hey, you yokels!" the coachman shouted, snapping his whip at them. "Why are you crawling like crabs in the middle of the road?"

They scattered out of the way, staggering like poisoned rats. Senderel in his haste slipped and fell; Benjamin collided with a market woman lugging a hamper of eggs, which instantly became so much matter for omelettes, whereupon she called curses down upon his head and all became bedlam. She went for the terrified Benjamin, flailed him with her arms and attempted to sink her claws in his beard. Benjamin was half dead by the time he managed to get loose from her clutches and take refuge in the blind alley into which Senderel had likewise run for cover.

"That's a big city for you!" the latter gasped, as he mopped the sweat from his face. "You musn't go here, you musn't stand there, or stop to rest anywhere. The devil alone can make these people out!"

"This is still something left over from the time of the Generation of Confusion," Benjamin said, seeking to explain away the incident. "Everything you see and witness here is characteristic of the Generation of Confusion, with its mad turmoil, its rapacity and outrageousness —"

"May the devil take them!" Senderel shook his hand in a futile gesture. "Come, Benjamin, let's rest up a bit. You look completely fagged, and your left cheek is as flaming as fire. May that trollop be accursed! Here, let me wipe your face — she splashed yolk all over your face!"

THE TINY congregation of one of Teterevka's humble synagogues was thrown into turmoil by the Crimean war, then in progress; overnight the congregation had split up into sundry factions, each at loggerheads with the others.

One clique, led by Heikel the Philosopher, favored Aunt Victoria, going to all lengths to glorify her astuteness and her ingenuity. Heikel had once been something of a watchmaker, was adept at perforating matzahs with a small indented roller and had no equal in erecting a *sukkah,** out of a noodle board, a baker's shovel, a dairy bench, the damper used to keep the *cholent*† hot over the Sabbath, a broken-down hencoop, and other such oddments, dovetailing everything most neatly and ingeniously. Therefore, when it came to mechanics, his views were held in high esteem.

"This subject is in Heikel's department," folks would say, as if to settle the matter.

Heikel had a way of telling stories about the ingenuity of English mechanical contraptions, stories so tall one simply couldn't believe one's own ears. And if one of his hearers interrupted him, demanding an explanation, Heikel would briefly say that the whole thing functioned

* The booth in which Jews live during the Feast of Tabernacles (*Sukkot*).
† A Sabbath dish.

by means of a tiny mainspring, at the same time giving a condescending smile, as if the whole vexing matter were thus cleared up. In short, according to Heikel the Philosopher, this mainspring was the prime mover for the clock, the telegraph, the music box and ever so many other amazing inventions.

Itzik the Hairsplitter, however, was never quite satisfied with these mainsprings of Heikel's. He considered them a heresy and would comment jeeringly: "Heikel will be telling us soon that the Golem and other such miracles and marvels of old were also operated by some tiny mainspring. *Pfui* — that's all I have to say to that! All the contraptions he brags about are — excuse me for saying so — nothing but plain rubbish."

Since Heikel the Philosopher had taken up the cudgels for Aunt Victoria, his relentless opponent, Itzik the Hairsplitter, stood up most valiantly for Aunt Rosa. The wrangling contenders moved heaven and earth to convert the other factions to their respective points of view. Once, when Heikel had well-nigh won over Shmulik the Carob Pod, the guiding light of the Uncle Ishmael clique, and had just about come to terms with Berel the Frenchman, a great admirer of Napoleon, Itzik the Hairsplitter formed a coalition with Tevyeh Mak, who was sponsoring Austria. A battle of words ensued, the synagogue strategists breathing fire and fury the like of which the congregants had not witnessed in decades.

It was at that crucial moment, at the height of Teterevka's battle royal, that our adventurers, seeking sanctuary, made their appearance in the House of Prayer.

Senderel, who was of a yielding rather than of a belligerent nature, nodded approval to the leader of each faction in turn.

"You want things that way?" he would say. "So be it, then. What do I care?" Consequently Senderel soon got on the right side of everybody. At the very first handshake folks recognized him as a man without guile, one who hadn't a stubborn streak in him. He could get along with anybody and everybody. Benjamin, on the other hand, had a severely critical temperament and was reluctant to endorse any one faction. Shortly afterward, however, he found Shmulik the Carob Pod quite to his liking and the two got on a friendly footing. It wasn't long before Benjamin had confided the secret of his proposed journey to Shmulik and the latter was greatly impressed. He conferred about it with Heikel the Philosopher, who pondered the matter a bit and, apparently convinced in turn, confided in Berel the Frenchman and in Tevyeh Mak. They all seemed profoundly impressed by Benjamin's unique project.

"Indeed," they all agreed, "this Benjamin doesn't seem to be an ordinary person. He's not of this world, somehow, with his head in the clouds; whenever he does say anything, there's no making him out. He's always woolgathering, staring at you with glassy eyes and grinning. His dress is sort of odd, and so's his behavior. All these things show that he's no ordinary mortal but belongs to some different category entirely. There *must* be something to him — there's more to him than meets the eye. Who knows? Perhaps this Benjamin is a reincarnation of someone else. You never can tell — "

One day when Benjamin and Senderel, all out of

breath, came into the synagogue, they found the assembled statesmen in an uproar, with Itzik the Hairsplitter orating at the top of his lungs, defying the rest of the politicos.

"Just see what's written in Yosippon!" Itzik said, jabbing his finger at an open page of a small volume. "It is written in Yosippon that Alexander of Macedon longed to behold the children of Jonadab, the son of Rechab; hence he marched with his heroic phalanx until he came to the Mountains of Darkness, where the sun never shines, and he and his myrmidons were unable to cross those mountains because the mire there was up to their knees. Do you grasp that? Alexander of Macedon, great Alexander himself, who soared on an eagle and had made his way to the very gates of the Garden of Eden — even he could not cross the Mountains of Darkness. So where does this nimcompoop, this Benjamin of yours, come in? Even Heikel with all his tiny springs couldn't help him one bit!"

"You blockhead, you!" Heikel plunged into the fray, poking his fingers into Itzik's shoulder. "Where are your eyes? Just see for yourself what's written right after that. 'Alexander of Macedon,' it says, 'heard the fowl of the air discoursing in Greek, and one bird spake unto him in these words: "Thy labors are all in vain, since what thou seekest is to come into the House of God, and into the house of His servants, the children of Abraham, Isaac and Jacob."' Now, you blockhead, do you grasp the reason why Alexander the Great couldn't cross those mountains?"

"But what will you do if it turns out, as some folks say

it will, that the Ten Lost Tribes, or the Sons of Moses, are dwelling somewhere close to the Land of Prester John? Well, let this creature of yours — begging his pardon — find that region. A fat chance!"

"*Teh*, what nonsense, Itzik! Really, now —"

"Hold on! Hold on, my great thinker! There's still a River Sambatyon in this world to be reckoned with! All right, let's assume that he does cross the Mountains of Darkness, and that he does find the Land of Prester John. Then he comes to the Sambatyon — and that's that! It keeps raining stones six days a week — there isn't a man living can get through and across! Even your Aunt Victoria with all her contraptions would be stumped, though she were to stand on her head!"

"Now, now! Are you starting up with Aunt Victoria again?"

"Really, Itzik, that's hardly fair of you — to speak ill of the kingdoms of the earth," flared up Berel the Frenchman. "Right now it's Benjamin we're discussing. Drag Benjamin through the mud to your heart's content, but don't go shoving your nose into the affairs of the kingdoms!"

"But why drag Benjamin through the mud?" Tevyeh Mak took up the cudgels. "It looks to me as if Benjamin is on the right track, which may yet lead to the deliverance of the Jews from their Exile — "

"You poor fish!" said Itzik the Hairsplitter, shrugging his shoulders. "I hardly expected you, of all people, to side with the others and to make such a fuss over this Benjamin. What you see in him is beyond me!"

"What we see in him, indeed!" Shmulik the Carob Pod mimicked him derisively. "Are you out of your head today, Itzik, or what? His very absent-mindedness, his indifference, his wandering gaze, and his peculiar behavior in general, ought to give you some idea of the man, one might think. If you can still disregard all that, I don't know how you go about appraising a real man! There, he has just come in. Please, do me a favor — go over and take a good look at him, and judge for yourself whether you aren't simply out of your mind. Well, Itzik, how do you feel about the whole matter now?"

Itzik advanced a few paces, surveyed Benjamin from top to toe, then spat in his face and stalked out in a huff.

A new political alignment resulted from the controversy revolving about Benjamin. Shmulik the Carob Pod and Berel the Frenchman joined forces with Heikel the Philosopher. Aunt Victoria launched an armada of one thousand ships freighted with ever so many terrifying contraptions. Uncle Ishmael crossed the River Prut, and Napoleon himself bombarded Sebastopol! Tevyeh Mak seemed to have lost his bearings and kept going round in circles, whereas Itzik the Hairsplitter was left strictly to himself. He nearly exhausted his entire bag of tricks and was almost beside himself in his one-man fight against all the others — no mere trifle that! However, he did vent his spite on Benjamin: from then on he haunted him, making his life miserable.

"As God is my witness," writes Benjamin, "I never mixed in politics. Because, first and foremost, what was the good of it? In the second place, what should Jews have to do with politics? So far as I was concerned, matters could have gone this way or that — it was all one to me. Senderel, too, steered clear of such affairs. Itzik, however, gave me no peace, day or night. He took delight in gluing feathers on the back of my coat, in throwing cushions at my head, or hiding now my right slipper, now my left. No sooner would I doze off in the synagogue than he would tickle the soles of my feet with a straw, or blow smoke up my nose through a paper squib. I would start awake, frightened out of my wits, coughing and wheezing from the vile smoke. . . . Was it my fault that all three factions had formed a cabal against him?"

THE GREATER part of each day our adventurers were busy plying their trade. As they made the rounds of Teterevka they got to be so well known in a short while that they were usually met with a smile, or some well-tried saw. Others in their place might have assumed a lofty manner and boasted of the special honors accorded them — of how people rejoiced at the mere sight of them and even at their casual remarks, and of the respect with which they were welcomed and escorted to the door. But the two were unassuming individuals and made light of the homage paid to them. Benjamin was engrossed in his main plan, while Senderel devoted all his energies to keeping his sack well filled and gathering a few extra coins for their travels. Whether the alms were given with a smile or with a frown, what did it matter, as long as his palm was crossed with silver, or even copper?

> Today is Purim, tomorrow no;
> Let's have that copper and let me go —

So runs that familiar and truly symbolic folk catch, which Senderel usually hummed during his wanderings from door to door.

"Good morning to you!" Senderel would greet the people upon entering a house; and, as he pulled Benjamin along, he whispered instructions in his ear about standing aloof and saying nothing, after which he would nudge him to one side.

Once, during their begging rounds, the two came upon a youthful competitor who was most voluble in trying to impress the master of a house. The young beggar grew more and more eloquent in soliciting a donation, producing some sort of a document that was supposed to attest to his worthiness. His prey, uneasy at being cornered and very anxious to escape the clutches of the shnorrer, hastened toward the two newcomers, hoping that they had come on real business. But when the true nature of their mission dawned on him, he was as stunned as a duck caught out in a thunderstorm.

"Some more travelers!" the master of the house growled, when he had recovered to some extent, and turning to the youngest one went on: "These fellows are travelers too! Heaven is raining travelers upon our heads today!"

The three petitioners exchanged glances.

"You know what?" Senderel whispered, tugging Benjamin's sleeve. "He's probably after the same thing we are — he might cut us out."

"It wouldn't surprise me a bit if you were all in cahoots," the master of the house conjectured.

"God forbid! God forbid!" Senderel and Benjamin protested in unison. "We're on our own —"

"You may go from here in peace, each one by himself, but you all strike me as one gang!" the householder said, growing impatient, and took out a coin.

"I beg your pardon, but please let me have that," Senderel said, stretching out his hand. "We'll give him his share. Come along, young man — I can change this."

Suddenly the door leading to the kitchen flew open and a shrill, angry voice issued out of it: "That's the one — that's the one, all right! The fellow standing near the other little skinny Jew. They're the same pair that were gawking along at that time. I recognize the lovely creature by his phiz and his sandy beard — may it be plucked out by the roots! I recognize him by his shirt, gaping at his throat! May he, please the Lord, be laid by his heels, and may his heathen bones be drained of their marrow!"

"Let's be going, Benjamin!" Senderel said, sensing danger. "May the devil take that wanton woman's father! Apparently she can't forget old scores; she still remembers those eggs you smashed —"

NOTHING MAKES sadder reading than the biographies of great men — how they endured great tribulations at the hands of the world for which they had sacrificed their lives and which they had enriched through their brilliant minds. The world, like a little child, prefers to jog along the trodden path, without the least deviation; it clings to its hoary folk tales and superstitions, repeated *ad nauseam* by the grandmothers and nurses, and thinks that there's nothing grander than the toys which it already has. The world clings to its accustomed ways, it is hostile to anything new, and heaps abuse on whoever attempts to alter the set pattern. It is only after the new idea has proven its worth that it is accepted and exploited to the full, while its poor promulgator is unceremoniously relegated to limbo. And if the world ever does remember to put up a monument for its great sons, it has a feeling of having more than fulfilled its obligations.

There are millions now living happily in America, yet Columbus, its discoverer, had plenty of grief in his time and was held up to scorn by his contemporaries. Our Benjamin of Tuneyadevka fared no better. His very appearance stamped him as an eccentric, and his talk of his projected journey elicited only mirth and derision. Fortunately for the world Benjamin didn't quite perceive the coolness of his reception; otherwise he might, God forbid, have become exasperated to the point of illness and abandoned his grandiose plans. And just think what the world would have lost then!

Consequently we shall omit numerous instances of the tricks that the people played on Benjamin, instances that would stigmatize men through all history; we'll pretend to ignore all these deplorable manifestations and simply go on with our story. "In Teterevka (writes Benjamin) there is a sizable community of Jews — may they be fruitful and multiply. Just who they are, and what their origin is, they know not. They have it on the word of their sires and grandsires that they are Jews and the descendants of Jews, and, to judge by their customs, their dress, and their language, they can be none other than Jews. Yet the community must be a conglomeration of diverse tribes, to judge by their prevailing indifference. If some man collapses in the street, no one will hasten to his aid, even though — may it befall only the enemies of Zion! — he be about to give up his ghost! There are those among them who are versed in the tongue of the gypsies — which is to say, they know how to read palms: they look into the hands of others and gain a living thereby, supplementing such earnings by their skill as lantern makers, wood turners and carpenters; the craftsmanship of some of them is truly to be admired. They are in addition gifted, by Him Whose Name is to be praised, with a ready rhyming wit, and on occasion they can move you to tears and melt your heart. These are, it is said, of Cretan stock.

"On the whole (Benjamin goes on), the townsmen are

honest, good folk. They always welcomed me cordially and seemed to derive a strange joy from my presence. It was quite evident that they were extraordinarily pleased with me. I wish, from the bottom of my heart, that God and men may be just as pleased with them. Amen!

"A most curious thing was (he writes) that one often came upon men in that region who had more than a streak of swinishness in them. One could detect this trait at a glance. Some maintain that this is due to a certain breed; others, that the natural conditions had something to do with it."

Benjamin himself did not wish to lean to either theory, since he held that matters of that nature were the province of those savants who devoted themselves to studying such things.

"Be that as it may (Benjamin continues), whether it is the one thing or the other, there is nothing new about this. We find it written in Delacrut's ancient volume, *The Image of the World:* 'There is a race in Brittany that has tails like animals, and in their midst one will come upon women tall and stalwart as Amazons, and their skins having bristles like unto those of swine. We also find mention of a horn-bearing race of humans in the land of the Franks; these mountains are inhabited by crookshanked women, and the more crookshanked a woman is the more beautiful she is accounted. Not unlike our own situation, since we have our share of women crookshanked and with other such points of allurement. The thing that hath been, it is that which shall be, saith the Preacher, and there is no new thing under the sun.

80

"Teterevka is a great city of magnificent buildings and long thoroughfares. At first sight it might strike one as a lively, bustling city, but when one becomes accustomed to it, one realizes that it is no more than a kind of Tuneyadevka on a larger scale. Its dwellers get up each day, eat, drink and go to bed again, the same as everywhere else. It keeps track of time by meals, and by the intervals between the meals. The three meals are the three oases of their lives, for which oases they yearn, even as cattle in a barren land yearn after lush pasture. It is the climate that is generally blamed for making its people lazy and drowsy. Whenever a man of great energy and large aspirations stumbles into this town and remains there for any length of time, he loses all his aspirations save those of sleeping, eating, drinking, and going to sleep again."

Teterevka was, in short, no more than one vast dormitory. Everything drowsed there: culture, trade, the banks, the very courts. And no matter how one strove to rouse its inhabitants, they remained sunk in slumber. Let but a few of them get together, and before you knew it they lost their power of speech, sat there yawning and staring listlessly at one another, and shortly all of them fell fast asleep. Only when supper was served were they awakened by the aroma, whereupon they devoured the food and — good night! — each crawled off home to resume his sleep.

In time our Benjamin began to yield to the same apathy. He found himself doing nothing more than eating and sleeping; his wanderlust had likewise become dormant. He was in extreme danger of being permanently beached and spending the rest of his mortal days there as a lotus eater, but, luckily for him, as well as for all mankind, a certain event occurred, which, like some great storm, impelled him on his course again.

Itzik the Hairsplitter's animosity toward Benjamin waxed greater with every day. His faultfinding redoubled and he taunted Benjamin, saying that the latter would reach the Sambatyon just about the time when figs would grow on thistles, and that he, Benjamin, would behold the Red Jews when he would be able to see his own ears.

But Benjamin refused to be ruffled, and solaced himself with soliloquies to the effect that our Creator will not let down those who have faith in Him. God willing, Benjamin felt that, despite all his enemies, he would reach his destination yet. And, when the spirit moved him, he would mutter a farrago of such things as *Great Viper, Lindenworm, the wild ass of the desert,* and so on, all of which was supposed to signify: "You'll still be yapping in envy, even as I shall be crossing the desert and nearing my goal."

Itzik would spit three times and declare that Benjamin had bees in his bonnet and ought to be taken to some country wizard. Things finally came to such a pass that no sooner would Benjamin appear in the street than gangs of guttersnipes would run after him, throwing stones and yelling "Lindenworm! Dragon!"

One day, as Benjamin and Senderel were out walking, a mob of boys came swarming down on them like locusts, so that the two had to take to their heels and seek refuge in one of the narrow back lanes. It ran downhill and they had to pass over a plank that bridged a runnel. Halfway over they almost collided with a man crossing from the opposite side. The only way to avoid him was to jump into the runnel at the risk of smashing their heads and probably breaking a leg or two, all of which they needed to continue on with their travels. And so Benjamin and Senderel stopped short and hung their heads.

"Ah! Peace be with you!" the man saluted them in a tone half humorous and half angry. "An opportune meeting, I must say! I couldn't have wished for a better!"

"Peace be with you, Reb Isaac David!" Benjamin mumbled in great confusion, for the one who had accosted him was none other than the sage of Tuneyadevka, Reb Isaac David the son of Reb Aaron Yossele.

"A fine pair!" Reb Isaac David chided them. "To sneak away from home like that, and for what reason? Is that any way to do things? What do you mean by sneaking off like that, and making deserted women of your wives? Riding roughshod over the law, irresponsibly, arbitrarily, against the laws of God and man. I'm asking you again: what have things come to? Just tell me: what brings you to these parts? And you too, Senderel — I can see you hiding behind Benjamin's back. Your wife, Senderel, will give you the hearty welcome you deserve, so she will! She is in such a rage, your wife is, that she could tear you in two like an overripe herring, so she could. Indeed, her heart told her that you must be here. And she insisted on coming along with me, did your wife."

"Ah! So he's here, is he?" a woman's voice shrilled behind Reb Isaac David. It didn't take Senderel long to recognize it as his wife's. Petrified with fear, he turned pale as a corpse and almost toppled off the plank, but managed to clutch at Benjamin's caftan in time. Everything swam before his eyes, and by now he could feel his spouse laying her hands upon him.

"Look at them, the two fine-feathered birds! Just look at them — may they both turn up their toes! Where is he, that scoundrel of mine — his name deserves to be blotted out — where is he? Let me at him for just a moment, so's I may show him there's a God in heaven!" Senderel's wife was screaming as she tried to push past Reb Isaac David.

"None of this yelling, and not so much noise!" Reb Isaac David tried to reason with her. "And no need to rush; you've been waiting so long, you can wait a bit more. You're no longer a deserted wife, since God has helped you. But — how does that saying go? — a woman will always be a woman. Shrewd, perhaps, but a woman just the same. Let us consider the question another way. After all, why all this fuss? Of course, it is galling to think that here's a man running away without a how-do-you-do or a by-your-leave, just so. But everything must proceed in an orderly fashion, I'll have you know. And since it has come to pass thus and so, then thus and so it is. And in that case, one asks: Why all this hubbub? However, it's still the same answer: Woman, forgive me for saying so, will always be woman!"

Reb Isaac David had just about warmed to his subject and was itching to thresh the whole matter out, taking it, after his wont, now on the one hand, now on the other, after which he would turn right around and season his

84

discourse with pepper and salt. But the crowd that by now had gathered at both ends of the bridge voiced their impatience with these people who had chosen — of all places! — to argue things out in the very middle of the plank, which could be crossed only in single file. The upshot was, Reb Isaac David and Senderel's wife had to turn back and let the others cross over. Benjamin and Senderel, for their part, lost no time in turning back as well.

"Please, Senderel, why are we standing here and what are we waiting for?" said Benjamin, who was the first to come to his senses. "We're standing here like babies tied with a string to the leg of a table! Now is our chance to give them the slip, foolish one!"

"Right you are, as true as I'm a Jew!" Senderel said, falling in with the suggestion and happy at the prospect of continued freedom. "Let's get going, unless you want to fall into her clutches again! That's not a mere plank-bridge, Benjamin — our ancestors in heaven have interceded to save us!"

Our travelers showed a clean pair of heels and within a matter of minutes were out of sight. Nor did they tarry long, but hastily got their things together and shook the dust of Teterevka from their feet.

"GEE, GEE up!" the driver of a covered oxcart bellowed hoarsely, almost running over two old women leisurely chatting right in the middle of the highway in Glupsk. The two, carrying small market baskets filled with meat, radishes, onions, garlic, and so on, had stood there exchanging local gossip and heartfelt confidences in whispers that could be heard a mile away. They scurried for their lives, and then, taking up their stations on opposite sides of the street, resumed their interrupted conversation, their voices drowning out the rumbling of the peasant carts constantly passing by.

"Well, Hassye-Beila, will you be there for sure tonight — at the fortuneteller's, I mean? I'll be there with my gentleman-friend. Yours will be there too — he asked me to tell you to come without fail. Come on, you'll have a good time, as sure as I'm alive. Well, what do you say, Hassye-Beila?"

"My mistress — may she burn! — wants to grant me the special privilege of kneading the dough tonight, and doing a few other such chores. But I'll manage to get out of them somehow and will try to come. But please keep this to yourself, Dobrish."

"Don't be in such a rush, Hassye-Beila! The cholera won't take your mistress if supper will be served an hour later. She wants to eat on time? The worms should eat her! Oh, I forgot to tell you, Hassye-Beila — be very careful in sifting the flour: watch out for the bran. Did you manage to make a few coppers on today's marketing, by any chance?"

"Stop, thief!" Hassye-Beila yelled at this point. "Stop the *shaigetz!* Snatching things right under your nose! Did you ever hear of anything like that?"

"What's the matter, Hassye-Beila? What are you yelling about?"

"A purse-snatcher, Dobrish! He nearly got away with my marketing bag — it's a good thing I saw him in time!"

"Look, Hassye-Beila! What's making the people run like that? Must be another fire — it's the second one today. I wouldn't be surprised to see a few more before nightfall."

"Why, I don't hear any fire bells. They'd be ringing if there was a fire."

"There comes Sima-Dvossye! She's got a finger in everything — I'll ask her. Sima-Dvossye, what's all the fuss about?"

"How should I know — may we know no sorrow! Perhaps Nehama Gisse knows. Nehama Gisse, darling, why are those people running as if they'd gone crazy? What did you say? Your geese and ducks are making so much noise I can't make out a word you're saying! Hodel gave birth today — she'll help you get rid of some of your ducks. You've got chickens, too? The price of eggs is so high today you can't touch them. What's going on over there?"

"How should I know? The Red Jews, or something — I've heard them yelling something about Red Jews."

"What? The Red Jews have come to town? My! my!

my! We've simply got to see them!" The women began clucking excitedly and bustled over to the gathering crowd.

"Hurrah for the dragon! Hurrah for the Lindenworm! Hurrah for the Red Jews!" the swarming urchins were shouting.

These Red Jews were none other than Benjamin and Senderel, who had made their way to Glupsk [Foolstown] and, in practically no time at all, had managed to gain celebrity. They had won the confidence of certain pious Jews, just as a miracle-mongering cobbler had done only a short time before.

Two crones, Toltza and Traina, pious souls who were known for their habit of trudging beyond the city limits every day at twilight, togged out in their best finery, as a reception committee for the Messiah if he should ever chance to come to Glupsk, had been lucky enough to come upon our wayfarers and to escort them into town. The pious souls had been immediately aware of their godsend. They nudged one another as they exchanged glances, as if to say: "*Nu*, Traina! *Nu*, Toltza! Our hearts had whispered the truth to us: these newcomers are no common mortals." They were proud of these wayfarers and actually felt rejuvenated. The venturousness of these travelers, their intention of exploring legendary regions, thrilled the two old women. When they had mended the travel-stained clothes of the two adventurers, the crones felt as happy as they had been in that distant time when they had been brides. In a word, our explorers had at last come upon fellow Jews who really appreciated them.

88

And it is only Glupsk that could truly appreciate and esteem so fine a pair!

Onward to Glupsk, you Jewish children! Why do you vegetate round the synagogue stove in your provincial towns? On to Glupsk, you sluggards, and may all the black years ensue for all things! There will you find your fellows — all the Toltzas and Trainas and other kosher souls who will welcome you heartily! There you can get ahead, give full scope to your talents, come into your own and know what life is really all about. On to Glupsk!

Benjamin — he that is Benjamin the Third, to be precise — has left us the following description of the town of Glupsk:

"First of all, when you arrive in Glupsk, by the road from Teterevka, you must leap over — I apologize for mentioning it — a mud hole; a little farther on you must leap over another, and still farther on a third, the largest of the lot, into which all the sewage of the town flows. If the gutters are filled with yellow sand used for scrubbing floors, with chicken and fish guts, with fish scales and chicken heads, you know it is Friday and time to go to the steam bath; if, on the other hand, they show egg shells, onion skins, radish parings, herring skeletons and sucked-out marrow bones — why, good Sabbath to you, you Jewish children!

"When you have got safely across the last mud hole, you will, my friends, come upon a mound of rubbish among the ruins of some hut or other, on top of which you will behold a cow, as placid as an itinerant preacher, chewing her cud and apathetically eyeing the passers-by as they breathlessly hurry every which way with their walking sticks and umbrellas. From time to time the animal will heave a soulful sigh, as though deploring the bitter lot of these passers-by and at the same time lamenting her own, for having fallen into the hands of some poor Jew or other. If you should happen — may it never come to pass! — to stub your toes against the jagged stones strewn all over the place, and, God forbid, trip and fall, you should, if you are at all able to do so, pick yourself up and go right on your way, until you come to a place that is the very heart of Glupsk. For if one may call the road from Teterevka the *stomach* of Glupsk, one can well designate its market place as its *heart*.

"A congeries of shops and stalls, throbbing with life, with hucksters crying their wares and crowds milling everywhere your eyes may turn. 'Get your pancakes here! Red hot!' — 'Hot buckwheat grits! Hurry, hurry!' The place swarms with shrilling ragamuffins. Now and then some of the Jews take time off for evening prayers, or to bless the new moon or to greet every passer-by with a 'Peace be with you, uncle!' There is a constant flow of porters girt with stout hempen ropes, weather-beaten veterans in shabby uniforms and boots with cracking tops, old-clothes men peddling every sort of rags. The muzhik watchman is planted stoutly in the middle of the square, eating with relish the heel of a white loaf he had been rewarded with for snuffing out the Sabbath candles, and is as careful as any pietist not to waste a crumb. Whenever there's a fair the thieves are right there — and there's no shortage of them here — they're prowling everywhere. A glum, disheveled young woman, desperately gesticulating, pops up to importune you for alms. Over there guttersnipes are hounding one of the town idiots, who is chanting heart-gripping folk songs, half in Yiddish, half in Polish. At another spot a young fellow with a peep show will allow you, upon payment of a copper, to see the sights of London, the Prussians scurrying like cockroaches before Napoleon, runaway horses upsetting a glittering phaeton with its important occupant, none other than a Pasha. Rows upon rows of country wives are squatting behind stalls heaped with garlic, cucumbers, gooseberries, currants, cherries and other fruit. Near the old ramshackle sentry box, which has lost its door and windows long ago, and around which the graybeards love to congregate and yarn about the past, sits Dvossia the market woman surrounded by troughs filled with fruit and vegetables; if it is wintertime you will find her squatting on a fire pot, like a setting hen on eggs."

There is a legend current in Glupsk, handed down from time immemorial, that some of the Jews whom King Solomon had sent on his ships to Ophir for gold and silver, elephants' teeth and apes and peacocks, had, for one reason or another, stayed on, going into trade and prospering. Later on, however, the wheel of fortune had turned and they had to escape. Of these, some had perished in the trackless desert, but others had managed to get safely out of the country and had embarked on Lake Pyatignilovka [Fivefold Foul], which in those days had been a river flowing directly into the ocean, and had sailed along without mishap for a space, until a tornado had smashed their ships to kindling wood and cast the exiles ashore. And on that spot the survivors had founded their city, and had named the city Glupsk.

The sages of Glupsk, known for their ingenuity in making mountains out of molehills, chasing wild geese and locating mares' nests, have, by drawing sundry inferences, by reading between the lines, shown that the legend is not without a considerable amount of truth. In corroboration of the soundness of their hypotheses, they pointed out the architectural pattern of the Glupsk houses, for one thing. Nowhere else on earth will you find the like of their dwellings, which look as if they had been built thousands of years ago and remind one of nothing so much as the round felt tents of Tartar nomads. There is nothing of symmetry or balance about them; the bizarre prevails. "Do you think your thatched-roof house is a monstrosity? Well, wait till you see mine; I'm building it on a zigzag plan, and if anybody doesn't consider it aesthetic enough, why, let him shut his eyes." Just as in the days of yore, as you see. In the second place, the customs of the dwellers in Glupsk do not differ greatly from those of the hoariest antiquity. Literacy and keeping of any written records is by no means general among them, so that public accounts are mostly kept in somebody's head, and the officials never have any concrete evidence to show — but, fortunately, they are never called upon, by anyone, to do so. Thirdly, the city's population is split up into clans or castes, not un-

like those of the Hindus. There is the Grab-All-You-Can
Clan, for instance, who may be considered the Brahmins,
ruling the town with an iron hand and without any
velvet-glove nonsense; then there are the Divvy-Ups,
guardians of that which was and is, fighting for both to
the last ditch — it consists of those who are on the public pay roll and who receive free provisions as well. There
are also the Connivers, who are only too glad to steer
you into a heap of trouble, without involving themselves
in the least. These, in turn, may be divided into sub-
castes: the Phony Bankrupts; the Rulers of the Market
Place; the Holier-Than-Thou Sinecurists, who put their
foot down in all matters of religion; those known as the
Foolish-Poltroonish-Voiceless Beggars are the pariahs and
untouchables, who shiver and shake and quiver and
quake before all the other castes and for reward have
the seven years' itch.

And last, but of course not least, there's the concrete
evidence of the coin that was unearthed during the con-
struction of a dam. This coin had been rubbed almost
smooth, but when examined very closely one could make
out on one side something like a rag of an apron tied to
a broomstick sticking up from a horse trough with some
people huddled on it and, on the reverse, ancient Hebrew characters corresponding to *J O S G S N L P.* The
archeologists of Glupsk long racked their brains over
this enigma, and naturally arrived at conclusions no two
of which agreed, until one savant hit upon the right in-
terpretation: the characters were the initial letters of
the legend: JEWS (from) OPHIR SAILED (to) GLUPSK (and)

93

SETTLED NEAR LAKE PYATIGNILOVKA. The broomstick, the apron, and the trough, he made it quite clear, represented the forefathers of the Glupskians sailing in a bark from Ophir. This savant wrote an elephant folio on his discovery, wherein he pleaded that Lake Pyatignilovka should be drained and its bed excavated in search of relics of antiquity. But the Glupskians would hear of no such thing, maintaining that whatever had been meant for consignment to eternal secrecy ought not to be brought into the light of day again.

Glupsk has a chain of some thirty or forty water holes (or mud holes, rather) running right through it, together with a number of flooded meadows; both meadows and water holes are connected with Lake Pyatignilovka by underground channels. With the coming of spring every last hole and meadow overflows and floods the whole town with mire so deep that even the tallest man, if he ventures out, has no trouble at all in getting the underside of his cap muddy. At nightfall the streets of Glupsk are lit by never less than one lantern, which burns the best of kerosene, and are guarded by two watchmen, each of whom has been serving faithfully for at least fifty years. But, just the same, people will persist in falling and breaking their arms and legs, while robberies are of quite frequent occurrence. All this, however, merely goes to prove that that which is fated to happen is bound to happen, and that neither watchmen nor the ingenuity of man can thwart destiny.

"That is why," Benjamin admonishes us, "we ought to close our eyes and place our trust in God, in the hope that come what may, He will bid His angels to guard us from evil. Could one, for instance, ask for better precautions than I bestowed on the bag holding my prayer shawl and phylacteries when I deposited it on a shelf right in the synagogue? And yet," Benjamin goes on, "when the Almighty refused to keep an eye on it, stolen from me it was, along with the rest of my belongings!"

WHEN THE two adventurers first saw Pyatignilovka they were lost in amazement. A lake such as that their eyes had never yet beheld! Senderel thought it the greatest expanse of water in the world. How could it be otherwise? Just think — it was at the very least a hundred times the size of the lake back in their Tuneyadevka. For Senderel was a simple, untutored soul who could only scratch his head over small print and was overawed by anything that went beyond the experience of Tuneyadevka. Benjamin, on the other hand, was a bit of a scholar; he had a taste of culture, had a smattering of the *Seven Wisdoms* and knew something about the Terrestrial Paradise, to say nothing of the ferocious creatures of remote India and such-like marvels; and though he, too, might stand spellbound before some novel sight, he had a way of smiling condescendingly, as if to say: "What folly! This isn't anything compared to the strange things lying ahead." Lake Pyatignilovka, he harangued Senderel, was no more, he should excuse the expression, than a puddle as compared with the Jordan, let's say. Lake Pyatignilovka would be no more than a drop if it came to slaking the thirst of the Wild Ox, which is preserved to feast the pious whenever the Messiah should come.

"You know what has occurred to me, Senderel?" Benjamin began, after contemplating the lake for a long while in silence. "Why can't we set out from here by water?"

"God be with you!" Senderel cried out in utter dismay. "Don't forget this, Benjamin: if the lake in our parts takes one life each year, how many lives must this endless expanse of water claim in the same interval? Spare our lives, Benjamin — take pity on your wife and children!"

"Faith! You must have faith, Senderel! Faith is second nature to the Jew! Having faith, our Father Jacob crossed the Jordan with nothing more than his staff; it is on faith alone, as you can see for yourself, that our fellow Jews open such huge stores. Everything about you is based solely on faith, and even many a great structure is reared, from basement to topmost story, on nothing but faith!"

"But just why do you wish to travel by water?" Senderel wanted to know, "when we can get to where we're going just as well by land?"

"I have a number of reasons," Benjamin explained. "First of all, I believe we can save both time and distance if we travel by water. We must reach our goal as soon as possible. Why? Delay exasperates one, Senderel; time is hanging heavy on my hands. If I could, I would wing my way there like a bird. In the second place, when Benjamin of Tudela, he that was Benjamin the First, started out on his voyage, he did so from Lake Ebro, as he plainly tells us in his book. If he chose to go by water in his day, let it be by water in ours. Rabbi Benjamin was in the world before us and was as farsighted as any of us — and so we must heed without question whatever he has to say."

"If that's the case," Senderel concurred, "it's the logical thing to do, Benjamin — as sure as I'm a Jew! And that applies not only to going by water — even if Rabbi Benjamin had traveled astride a broomstick, we oughtn't to hesitate to set out on broomsticks as well!"

"And in the third place," said Benjamin, cutting Senderel short, "it won't do any harm for us to grow accustomed to traveling by water before we come to crossing the great stormy sea, Oceanus itself. In fact, before we wind up our affairs here in Glupsk, it might actually be advisable to take a trip on this lake. There's a man with a boat over there. Let's offer him a coin and ask him to take us for a boat ride."

And, within a minute or two, our adventurers, fortified by faith, stepped into the rowboat and started off over the lake. At first both shrank in fear. Senderel, dizzy and trembling from head to foot, was afraid that the boat would capsize, leaving his wife a wretched widow.

"Don't fret so much about your dizziness," Benjamin said, trying to brace him up. "Everybody suffers from seasickness on his first sea voyage. Next time, you'll see, you won't feel so bad."

After crisscrossing the lake several times, however, and taking delight therein, so emboldened did the two adventurers become that crossing the ocean itself seemed but a trifling matter to them. Benjamin, with Senderel interpreting, bombarded the boatman with questions.

"Ask the captain, Senderel, how far it is from here to the sea itself? Ask him if there are any islands on that sea and, if so, what people live on them? Are there any of our brethren among them? Who collects taxes from them, and have they tasted the taste of Exile? Or you might ask the Gentile, Senderel, just for curiosity's sake, where the Nisbon Mountains are and ask him about the infidel Turks. Or anything about the Ten Lost Tribes. You can never tell — he may have heard something or other."

However, the smattering of Russian Senderel had acquired in helping his spouse to drive bargains for eggs, onions and potatoes, fell far short when it came to discussing such erudite topics with a master mariner. Senderel was a sorry sight as he struggled to make himself understood, gesticulating not only with his hands but with his feet and, God have mercy on him, actually breaking into a cold sweat. The captain merely became more and more impatient, spitting in disgust and eyeing Senderel malevolently as the latter floundered and stared helplessly into the other's eye.

"He's asking about the Red Jews, he is," shouted Senderel in desperation, gesturing piteously toward Benjamin.

"The only redheaded Jews I know are Leibka and Shmulka — both of them rich," the boatman answered, in his simplicity.

"No, not Leibka — no, no! He's asking about the Red Jews 'way over there — how shall I say it? — near Mount Nisbon. That's what he's asking about!"

"Nisbon — a Jew by the name of Nisbon?"

"Tell him it's a mountain, Senderel!" Benjamin broke in. "Go on, tell him — explain to him what a mountain is!"

Fluttering his hands in the air, in an effort to describe a mountain, Senderel kept shouting: "High! Very high!"

But the Gentile, by now thoroughly aroused, merely

99

spat again and mumbled something under his breath about pestering devils.

Benjamin had many wonderful stories to tell about his adventurous voyage on Lake Pyatignilovka, which were subsequently to become so celebrated throughout the civilized world. Here we can give you but a few of them. At one point, as he was being rowed across the lake, his attention was caught by a large patch in its very center, overgrown with vivid greenery. Confident that he had come upon an island carpeted with fragrant herbiage, he put one foot overboard, preparing to leap ashore, when the boatman caught him by his coattails and drew him back into the boat with such force that he fell and lay there in a daze for quite a while. He was oblivious even to the raging billows as the boat struggled onward. When he came to, the Gentile informed him that he would most likely have drowned: the patch of vivid green wasn't an island at all but merely the thick scum that blanketed Pyatignilovka Lake every year at this season.

"I, however (Benjamin tells us) could not accede to the view that it was really scum. True, there was a certain odor about it, but I had never heard, nor read in my books, of water being blanketed with such greenery. If there had ever been anything of the kind, some sort of fruit would have been bound to grow thereon and a new benediction, something like 'Blessed Be the Creator of the Fruit of the Water,' would necessarily have had to be devised! No; I am inclined to believe that this was the sea monster, Kileyna, referred to as follows in *The Image of the World:* 'This monstrously huge fish becomes so encrusted with earth and grass that it takes on the aspect of an island. Voyagers, cruising by and deceived by its appearance, often beach their boats upon its back and even kindle a fire to cook their food. When the Kileyna feels the penetrating heat, however, it dives to the very bottom of the ocean and all those encamped upon it find a watery grave.' This merely corroborates the views of those masterminds who maintain that the inhabitants of Glupsk had originally come from Ophir: while sailing from that remote region, in the dim past, their bark had been followed by this sea monster, right into Lake Pyatignilovka!"

At another spot Benjamin chanced to discern, at the bottom of the lake, figures that looked very much like those of women.

"Long, long ago I had read somewhere about mermaids," he writes. "The author of *The Image of the World* bears true testimony: 'Their heads, their torsos and their breasts are those of virgins; they sing most sweetly and are called sirens.' Also, trustworthy persons of venerable years have testified to having seen such mermaids in show booths at fairs. But now I had come to see them with my own eyes. When I drew the attention of our captain to those wonderful water nymphs, he merely pointed out certain peasant women who were washing linen on the shore. I kept pointing to the bottom of the lake, but he, with equal persistence, kept pointing to the shore. Since I could not make myself clear in his language, neither of us could grasp what the other was trying to explain. . . ."

One afternoon our wayfarers were strolling at some

little distance beyond the town, chattering and laughing, as happy as thrushes or newlyweds; each took delight in the other's every word or gesture. What made them so happy? Why were they carrying on as though they weren't quite right in their heads? Well, they had resolved, without actually making any vow, to leave Glupsk the very next day and, in a propitious hour, to set sail for the goal beckoning to them.

As they were strolling along in this merry mood, they were overtaken by two Jews driving by in a peasant cart, one of whom was lolling back with his cap tilted to one side and chewing on a straw — the marks of a deep thinker engrossed in hatching some super-scheme. Taking in the pedestrians at a glance, the men in the cart engaged them in talk, putting all the inevitable questions: Where did the two hail from? What were their names? Benjamin and Senderel needed little urging to become quite talkative — whatever was in their hearts was on the tip of their tongues. The two in the cart grinned meaningfully, winking at each other, while the one chewing on the straw whispered to his companion: "Well, they're as good as ours; if worst comes to worst we'll only be out a few coppers." Then, turning to the strollers: "You know what?" he began. "Our city also deserves the honor of a visit from two such eminent fellow Jews. We are inviting you right here and now to come along with us. Do us that honor, friends, and don't hesitate. We can assure you that our community will extend you a fitting reception, and will dine and wine you."

"We would gladly go along with you," Benjamin temporized, "but we've decided — without actually vowing — to set out from here by water, early tomorrow morning."

"Excuse me for saying so," the other persisted, "but this is utterly childish talk. Whoever heard of Lake Pyatignilovka? It's no more than a mud hole, a stagnant pond covered with green scum, as compared with our own Dnieper, which flows right into the Black Sea. And in that way, God willing, you will reach your destination much sooner. Don't be so stubborn — jump in and let's start."

"What's your opinion?" Benjamin turned to Senderel. "Should we follow their suggestion, perhaps, and go along with them?"

"What do I care?" Senderel responded. "If you want it so, so be it!"

Tired with walking, and elated at this unexpected good fortune, the two were only too glad to stumble into the cart. From then on their hosts kept an eagle eye on them, but at the same time plied them with food and wine, and pampered them as women in a delicate condition are pampered, and this treatment suited the two adventurers to a *t*.

Next day, toward evening, they arrived safe and sound at Dnieprovitz, where they were lodged at an inn and were treated to a hearty supper.

"You seem tired; better go to bed early and have a good rest," their entertainers told them. "Tomorrow, God willing, we'll conduct you to some of our leading citizens and introduce you properly. They will not only welcome you but take care of all your needs and enable you to proceed on your journey. Good night!"

"Good night to you! And a good year!" Benjamin and Senderel answered in unison.

They lost no time in reciting their prayers and then, yawning and scratching themselves a bit, dozed off in contentment.

"HAVE MERCY upon me! At least give me time enough to make my deathbed confession!" Senderel cried out in a nightmare, awakening Benjamin. The latter, not knowing if he were dead or alive, jumped to his feet and tried to find out what was wrong with his companion.

Outside the windows black night was yielding to the gray of dawn; everything was still as death. But indoors the sleepers were snoring away, each after his temperament: one twanging like a banjo, another blaring like a trumpet, still another indulging in a muted staccato, and a fourth going off into a high-pitched crescendo, switching to a querulous, questioning note and winding up with a tattoo, for all the world as if his puffing cheeks were a drum. Together they formed a sort of nasal orchestra, playing a symphony in honor of the celebrated Dnieprovitz bedbugs who were feasting upon the flesh and blood of the sleepers — good Jewish blood and good Jewish flesh. The lowly, out-of-the-way Dnieprovitz inn feasted its man-eating bedbugs for a long time. Every Jewish guest had anticipated paying blood money, as it were; there was no wriggling out of it, but still, every now and then one of them would murmur in sleepy protest: "There, you Dnieprovitzer, you've had your fill — now begone!"

"What are you yelling about, Senderel?" Benjamin

questioned his companion who was still half asleep. "It must have been one of those bedbugs — my, this place is overrun with them! I couldn't sleep a wink all night."

"Let's clear out of here as fast as we can," the drowsy Senderel mumbled.

"God be with you, Senderel! What on earth are you trying to say? Suppose a bedbug did bite you? The creature doesn't know any better, but you — you are a man — "

Senderel stared at him glassily for an instant and then sighed: "My, what a terrible dream I had! May it never come true!"

"*Teh,* a man has all sorts of dreams, at one time or another!" said Benjamin, trying to soothe him. "I, for instance, dreamt tonight that a dragon had spotted me, looked me over, and then said to me: 'I beg your pardon, but will you please follow me? Alexander of Macedon is bivouacking over yonder with his phalanxes and is anxious to meet you.' Then the monster wheeled about and broke into a gallop, and I started running after him. 'You're rushing — may you be spared the evil eye — as if to outstrip the wind. I can hardly keep up with you!' I heard someone calling behind me. I turned round — and whom did I see but Alexander of Macedon. 'My Lord King!' I cried out, grabbing his hand and squeezing it hard — when suddenly there was a sharp stench in my nostrils, so overpowering that I all but fainted. And when I awoke, a bedbug was crushed in my hand. *Pfui!* Listen to me: spit three times over your shoulder, and forget you ever had a nightmare. What was it all about?"

"*Pfui, pfui, pfui!*" Senderel dutifully spat thrice and proceeded to recount his dream:

"I dreamt that I was out for a stroll and when I'd gone some distance I was suddenly grabbed from behind, thrown into a sack and carried off. Then someone untied the sack and fetched me such a wallop — and I mean a wallop — that two of my teeth were knocked loose! 'That's just by way of a deposit,' someone assured me. 'The rest you'll get by and by!' I turned round — and who should be standing there but my wife, wearing a nightcap and frothing at the mouth, all set to pounce on me. 'You just wait a second, my darling husband,' said she, ever so sarcastically, 'I'm going to fetch the bread-shovel and prove to you that we still have a God in heaven.' No sooner did she go out to get the shovel than I was off like a shot, and I didn't stop until I'd come to some sort of an inn. It was all dark, the floor was slippery, and there wasn't a soul stirring there. I stretched out in a corner and dozed off. And as I lay sleeping there, my grandfather, Reb Senderel of blessed memory, appeared before me; all in tears and with his head cast down, he urged me: 'Wake up, Senderel, my son! As God is dear to you, Senderel, arise and take thyself off, wherever your eyes may lead you! You're in dire peril!' So I tried to get to my feet but could hardly stir, as if somebody — or something — were holding me back. I clutched at my head — and I came on a mobcap. Ho-ho! I wasn't Senderel at all, but — excuse my saying it — some housewife or other, without a trace of a beard, wearing a woman's jacket, and my belly — may all Jews be spared such a thing! — full of shooting pains. 'Don't be so alarmed,' someone soothed me, 'things are always a little more difficult with a first-born —' 'Oh, uncle, uncle!' I screamed with pain. 'I can't stand it, I feel I'm going to faint at any moment.' 'A good blow on the nape of your neck would be the best medicine for you,' some uncle or other commented and, without further ado, swung at me. 'That'll hold you for the present — and for what has come before, and for what's still to come!' he snapped at me, and vanished.

"I just lay there for a while in agony, until, with God's help, I mustered strength enough to get up. I tried to open the door, but all my banging didn't do any good. But then the door suddenly swung open, and as I put my foot over the threshold I was seized by some cutthroat and dragged off to a cave. When we got there they whipped out a slaughterer's knife and tried to kill me. As the knife was poised above my throat I managed to scream: 'Have mercy upon me! At least give me time enough to make my deathbed confession!' There, that's the whole story, Benjamin. May it all turn out for the best!"

"Spit three times, Senderel," Benjamin counseled him again, "and drive those nightmares out of your head. Moreover, since it's already daybreak, you may as well get up and recite a few Psalms."

Heaving a deep sigh, Senderel left his bed, washed his hands perfunctorily, put on his gabardine, and, fetching forth the Book of Psalms, turned back to where he had left off and proceeded to intone the Tenth Psalm lugubriously:

"Why standest Thou afar off, O Lord?
Why hidest Thou Thyself in times of trouble? . . ."

His chanting took on a more somber and emotional tone:

"For the wicked boasteth of his heart's desire,
And the covetous vaunteth himself, though he con-
    temn the Lord. . . .
He sitteth in the lurking-places of the villages;
In secret places doth he slay the innocent;
His eyes are on the watch for the helpless.
He lieth in wait in a secret place as a lion in his lair,
He lieth in wait to catch the poor;
He doth catch the poor, when he draweth him up
    in his net."

By the time Senderel had done chanting it was broad daylight and everybody was up and about. A huge samovar stood steaming on the table and tea was passed round. It seemed to have a salutary effect upon Benjamin and Senderel. The room, which had served as a bedchamber during the night and as a teahouse in the morning, was shortly transformed into a House of Prayer. One could see sleeves being rolled up everywhere, exposing every variety of Jewish arm: hairy and smooth, gaunt and stout, dark-skinned and pale. The worshippers quickly put on prayer shawls and phylacteries and began the morning service. Benjamin and Senderel, though still travel-weary, recited their prayers with ardor, swaying to and fro, their chanting emanating from the very depths of their woebegone hearts.

The prayers over, each participant took a sip of his noggin of brandy, smacked his lips, saluted all the others with a "To your health!" and expressed the wish that the Creator of the Universe might have mercy on His poor flock, and then with a suppressed sigh, downed the rest of his drink. No run-of-the-mill Jews, these, but pious and dignified.

One of these dignified Jews, who had brought our friends to the inn, went away and was absent for two hours or so. Upon his return he and his companion exchanged meaningful glances and both seemed to be exceedingly pleased by something. Before long they ordered the table to be set, proceeded to wash their hands, without forgetting to examine the copper dipper, as behooves pious Jews, and invited their two guests to join them in their repast. They were in high spirits, praised the culinary skill of the hostess, and debated the fate of world Jewry; it was high time for their weary brethren to be redeemed, and they showered praises on God's Chosen People.

"Wherein have the Jews been weighed in the balance and found wanting? They excel in all sciences and inventions, from the telegraph and railroad — in everything. But such things are secondary. What matters most is the innermost core, the essence of a Jew," one of them rambled on. The heretics, the ultramodern philosophers, came in for severe censure and a tirade was leveled at the secular schools where heresy was tolerated and Jews went bare-headed.

"We hope that the Lord, all praise be His, may prove

merciful," said the speaker, at long last turning to our adventurers, "and fulfil everything that we wish for you."

Benjamin rejoiced at such a blessing.

"You know what, Reb Benjamin and Reb Senderel?" their entertainers concluded, getting up. "Let's act simply and unceremoniously, in accordance with the ways of our fathers. A journey should be followed by a visit to the baths. A sweat bath drives away fatigue and all aches. You can also get your hair cut there, if you wish. After that we'll attend to our main business."

No Jew will ever turn down an invitation to the bathhouse. What a pothouse is to a muzhik, what a pond is to a duck, the bathhouse is to a Jew, only a hundredfold more so. The enjoyment a Jew derives from a steam bath cannot be fathomed by any other race or nation. The bath is in a great measure associated with his religion, with his inner life, and even with his marriage customs. You could not make a Jewish soul stir from heaven to take on human form, you could not entice it down to earth by any other lure save that of the sweat bath. For it is an intermediate stage, a sort of halfway house between heaven and earth. Long before a Jew is born word of the blessed event will get round by the bathhouse grapevine; a Jew would find no delight in his soul on the Sabbath and on festivals, were it not for the preliminary steaming. Look at a Jew returning from the baths on the eve of Sabbath: he has a sprightlier gait, all his senses are on the alert, and his nostrils find the aroma of *gefilte fish* more tantalizing than ever. He will chant the Song of Songs like any nightingale (well, almost), and is, on the whole, transported to celestial climes. He comes to the bathhouse as though to his fatherland — a realm where all men are free and equal, and there he reaches a high level — the highest ledge in the steam room.

Consequently Benjamin and Senderel readily fell in with the proposal, and joined their entertainers without any misgivings. They knew that all bathhouses were equally unprepossessing and weather-beaten, and usually situated in some out-of-the-way, hard-to-reach quarter. Our heroes were therefore spellbound when their guides brought them to an imposing three-story structure in the very heart of town.

"Is this a bathhouse?" Senderel timorously asked.

"It's easy to see you're from the country. Step inside and you'll see something still better!"

When they entered, the adventurers came to an abrupt halt, fascinated by the glistening parquet floors and glossy rugs, so much like those of the enchanted palaces described in fairy tales. Who could tell — perhaps some princesses might actually appear to welcome them? However, it was only a soldier who approached — and bade them undress.

"Yes, do that," one of their hosts seconded emphatically. "In the meanwhile we'll go and pay for you. You'll certainly sweat plenty!"

When Benjamin and Senderel had stripped, they picked up their shabby clothes expecting to do a little laundering while steaming themselves: having brought no extra linen with them, their underwear was sadly in need of a washing by now. But the sentry unceremoniously took their tatters away and led them into an ornately decorated room, where several well-dressed men, some of them in uniform, were seated round a huge mahogany table. The two naked men looked about them in surprise, at a loss to explain the absence of steam in this room, or even any means, such as heated stones, for generating steam.

Senderel, prompted by Benjamin, gave voice to his doubts: "Is this a Jewish bathhouse?"

One of the men at the table approached them, cast a glance at their starved bodies, and made a remark in Russian.

"Eh? What's he saying, Senderel?" Benjamin asked in curiosity.

"I can't make out a word of it!" Senderel said, shrugging his shoulders. "What a language! 'Your ticket!' he says — something about a ticket."

"What's there to understand, foolish one?" Benjamin tried to set him at ease. "He must be the proprietor, and he's demanding our admission tickets: you have to show a ticket to enter a bathhouse such as this. Just tell him that our friends went to pay for us."

"Those other Jews, you see, sir — they have already paid for us," Senderel tried to speak up, jabbing a thumb over his shoulder, but all further explanation stuck in his throat.

"What you mean, sir? They already pay," said Benjamin, trying in his pidgin Russian to clear up the matter once and for all.

The official motioned to the guard, and the pair were whisked off into another room. The two bewildered victims were still hoping to get their longed-for steam bath.

Later on, when the two hapless fellows were marched out into the street, they were almost unrecognizable. Their beards and earlocks were gone, their brows were beaded with cold sweat, they were bowed and crestfallen because of the sudden turn of events; they trudged along miserably in the midst of a convoy.

Dark, threatening clouds now moved swiftly across the overcast sky, followed by thunder and lightning. A strong wind sprang up, its whirling gusts picking up dust, leaves and all sorts of rubbish and making them all swirl in a dance of death. . . . A cloudburst flooded the whole region; the very heavens wept in sympathy with the despair of our woebegone travelers, and the raindrops mingled with their tears.

Alas! Benjamin and Senderel had not been forewarned that it is not only in the desert that travel is fraught with danger, because of its beasts of prey, its Dragon-Vipers and kindred perils; they were unaware of the even greater dangers lurking in the densely populated communities. It was during an evil, sorry time that our travelers had ventured forth — a time when one Jew would lie in wait to catch another, one without a passport, and deliver him over into the hands of the military authorities, as a sacrificial offering to obtain exemption for a son, or the son of a friend. Alas! Our unfortunate adventurers did not realize that they were, to all intents and purposes, in a desert infested with beasts of prey, and that the two imposing fellow Jews were in reality but two-legged Dragon-Vipers.

THE BITTER, unenviable lot of our crushed heroes need
not be dwelt upon. At first they were utterly bewildered,
unable to account for the sudden change in their fortunes. Everything about them was strange and grotesque: the barracks, the other soldiers, the language,
and the rudiments of military drill. Their uniforms
draped them with all the gracefulness of sacks, their caps
were tilted at a ludicrous angle. To the casual beholder
the whole thing appeared farcical: the pair looked like
scarecrows got up to parody soldiers and to burlesque
military bravado. Pitiful was the fate of any rifle that fell
into the hands of either of the two recruits: they handled
their weapons with all the dexterity of butter-fingered
cook's helpers working with bread-shovels. Their drilling
was one endless comedy and, needless to say, they came
in for their share of resounding blows. However, is there
in this world any misfortune to which man can't grow
inured? And not man alone. Take a bird, for instance —
the most foot-loose and fancy-free of creatures in the
world. Cage it, and it becomes reconciled to captivity,
pecks at the birdseed eagerly enough, hops around and
chirps quite merrily, as if the woodland and the great
open spaces were still at its disposal. Senderel, little by
little, became accustomed to his lot. After observing
other soldiers being put through their paces, he would

attempt to go the drill all by himself, strutting as proudly as any tom turkey whenever he managed to execute any part of it, no matter how clumsily, and even though he was staggering and ready to fall at the very end. Benjamin's wounds, on the other hand, would not heal over; he was one of those freedom-loving birds that, at the first frost, migrate to warmer climes. Denied freedom, such a bird loses its appetite, grows moody, and yearns with all its being to escape. The journey he had planned, and because of which he had deserted wife and children, had apparently cast a spell over him and now deprived him of any peace of mind. And so Benjamin passed a winter of indescribable misery.

One day when spring had arrived at last, Benjamin came up to Senderel as the latter was drilling by himself:

"Upon my word, Senderel, you're clowning like a street urchin! What good will it do? Don't forget — praised be the Lord! — that you're a married man, after all, and a Jew. Why do you bother with things like that, let alone putting your heart into it? What does it matter, I ask you, whether you 'about face' with your left foot or your right?"

"How should I know? They tell me 'About Face!' — so 'About Face!' let it be! What do I care?"

"And what about our journey? Heaven! What about our journey to the uttermost ends of the earth — have you forgotten about it already?" asked Benjamin with renewed fervor.

"Hup! Hup! Hup!" Senderel started goose-stepping.

"Woe unto thee, Senderel, and woe unto thy 'Hup!'

Pfui! You ought to be ashamed of yourself! Just tell me this: shall we ever start out on our journey again?"

"We could start out today, for all of me!" Senderel responded. "If they'd only let us go!"

"Of what use are we to them, and what do we need them for?" Benjamin said, trying to enlighten him. "Upon your word as a Jew, Senderel: were the enemy, God forbid, to appear — would the two of us stop him? And if you were to warn the enemy a thousand times over: 'Go away, or I'll go *bing, bing, bang!*' — would he take the least heed of you? I should say not! He'd grab hold of you and you'd be lucky to get out of his clutches with a whole skin. Believe me, the way I see things, we're not worth a row of pins to our officers, and they'd be only too glad to get rid of us. With my own ears I've heard the commanding officer say that we're nothing but a nuisance, and if it were up to him he'd send us packing to where all the years are black. I tell you it was all a mistake, a ridiculous blunder, from the very start. We're not their kind and they're not ours. Those who delivered us into their clutches must have told them that we were men of valor and familiar with all the arts of war. Is it our fault if those men were liars? Weren't they liars to us as well? I'll take my oath on it, in prayer shawl and with my shroud on, that the matter of waging wars never even entered into our conversations with them. We came here merely to scrape a few coppers together before going on our way. But if we're simply to be abducted, to be sold into bondage, then all authority and justice are at an end. It's all the fault of those two Jews, those scoundrels, who deceived not only us but the others!"

"Well, what's to be done now, Benjamin?"

"We ought to proceed on our way. I don't think any-one will stop us — by right, no one can stand in our way. And if you're afraid that they won't let us go, well, there's a way of getting round that: let's give them the slip. Who has to know our business? Do we have to bid them good-bye when we leave?"

"That's what I think, too; there's no need of any leave-takings," Senderel agreed. "Did we say as much as a goodbye to our families when we left home?"

Our two warriors took to pondering plans for their escape. Benjamin was all on edge again, woolgathering as he walked about. He was oblivious to the pain even when he was cuffed for neglecting to salute some officer; if he was reprimanded for some infraction of discipline, he would be on his toes for just about as long as the lax Jews of Chernovitz are during the rather lengthy recital of the Scroll of Esther in their synagogues. The prospective journey claimed his undivided attention.

And so, late one night, when the men in the barracks were all sound asleep, Benjamin tiptoed over to Sen-derel's bunk and whispered: "Are you ready, Senderel?"

Senderel nodded, even though they were in the dark, and, holding on to his companion, slunk out with him. They were greeted by a warm breeze; murky clouds were moving across the sky in unbroken succession, like an endless file of loaded peasant carts hastening to some fair in heaven. The moon seemed to be tagging along with this bizarre caravan, peeping out every now and then to see if everything were going well, and then withdrawing to its ethereal heights.

They clambered up a woodpile and from there got atop the fence. Suddenly Senderel clutched at Benjamin's sleeve and whispered uneasily in his ear: "I forgot something! I forgot the sack. Should I go back for it?"

"God forbid! If God helps a man to escape, He will also provide him with a new sack!"

"It's my grandfather — of blessed memory — that I'm thinking of now," Senderel spoke softly. "He warned me in my dream: 'Wake up, Senderel, and run for your very life!' May his merits intercede for me now! Grandmother, peace be unto her, used to say —"

But before he could tell Benjamin just what it was his grandmother used to say, they caught the sound of a sentry approaching. They hugged the fence and held their breath. When the sentry had passed at last, the two spectral figures crept along on all fours, until they were comparatively safe.

"Grandmother, peace be unto her," Senderel resumed, "used to say that Grandfather, of blessed memory, had yearned all his life long to go to the Holy Land, and that just before he was gathered unto his fathers he had cried out: 'I have not been found worthy in the eyes of the Lord, it seems! But I have faith that one of my line will reach there!' And I have a feeling that it was me he meant. May the Lord pay heed!"

But it was other than divine ears which Senderel's words reached. He had hardly finished when they heard the challenge "Who goes there?" delivered in ringing Russian. Receiving no answer, the sentry advanced a step or two. And, as ill-luck would have it, the moon had to put out her head from behind a dark cloud just then, shedding her full light on our adventurers, who, frightened out of their wits, were standing stock-still while the sentry cursed them and threatened them with his gun.

In a matter of minutes both were under arrest.

Words cannot suffice to describe the troubles the two prisoners underwent. They became all skin and bones and looked like wizened old men. Senderel, at least, managed to put in several hours of sleep each day, and thus forget his troubles; now and then he would be rewarded with a pleasant dream; his grandfather, Reb Senderel, took to visiting him more and more often, consoling him each time. Nor did he ever come with empty hands. Sometimes it was a toy bow and arrow he brought his grandson, at other times it would be a wooden sword or a Haman rattle. He would smile and pinch his grandson's cheek and say: "Here are some toys for you, my little one! Make them go *bing, bing, bang!*" And once he brought along a teetotum, which the grandson kept twirling until he had won a copper from his granddaddy. A good dream, no matter what you say, is not without its advantages. However, isn't the whole world but a dream? Benjamin, however, because of his insomnia, was deprived even of such consolation. He chafed under his restraint. He could see the sunshine from the prison windows, and the green grass, trees in full bloom, people strolling about and birds wheeling against the sky. Wanderlust seized upon him again — it was high time he took to the road again, but there he was imprisoned and farther than ever from his journey's end. In his agony he fidgeted about, clutched at his head and murmured: "What harm did I ever do them! Good God, what do they want of me?"

SOME TIME after their arrest, a court-martial — its personnel including not only a colonel but a real live general, and all of them in full uniform — was convened in the regimental headquarters. Standing near the doorway were two woebegone creatures, their heads cast down and looking more like rats that had narrowly escaped drowning in an earthen mug of buttermilk than a pair of deserters. The officers scrutinized them, grinned, and exchanged whispers.

"You know what, Senderel?" one soldier said under his breath to the other. "Even if I knew my death, God forbid, was awaiting me in this room, I am bound to tell them the whole truth — that's how worked up I am!"

"Go ahead and tell them the truth, Benjamin, for all of me! What do I care?" answered the other desperado.

"Are you the two charged with leaving the barracks at night without official leave?" the general asked them in a stern voice. "Are you aware of the penalty for such an act?"

Benjamin, placing his trust in God, plunged into his defense, half in Yiddish, half in Russian, in a manner that would have more than done credit even to Heikel the Stammerer of Tuneyadevka.

The general turned away to conceal his smile, with an "I give it up!" gesture, whereupon the colonel took over.

"The two of you are guilty of an offense deserving the severest punishment!" he declared in a thunderous tone.

"Your honor!" Benjamin vociferated. "Trapping people in broad daylight and then selling them like chickens in the market place — that's permissible? But when these same people try to escape, you call it a crime? If that's the case, the world must be coming to an end and I fail to understand what you call 'permissible' or 'not permissible'! No, let's ask all those here, and let them say who's in the wrong! Suppose, Your Honor, that you had been waylaid somewhere on the road and a sack was thrown over your head — would you call it a crime if you were to escape from that sack? This, I'm telling you, was nothing but a case of kidnapping and downright fraud — we were taken in, and so were you. The only ones to blame, I'll have you know, are the two treacherous swindlers who got us into this mess! Speak up, Senderel — don't stand there like a golem! Come out with God's own truth, and shame the devil! And say together with me: 'We want to tell you that we don't know a thing about waging war, that we never did know, and never want to know. We are, praised be the Lord, married men; our thoughts are devoted to other things; we haven't the least interest in anything having to do with war. Now, then, what do you want with us? You yourselves ought to be glad to get rid of us, I should think!' "

Benjamin had hit the nail on the head: the army had been yearning for a long time to get rid of them. Whenever their superiors had observed the untidy appearance, the clumsy marching and the awkward behavior of the pair, they would roar with laughter and wonder how the two had ever been mustered into the service. The court-martial merely went through the motions. The way Benjamin and Senderel had conducted themselves throughout the inquiry had, the Lord be praised, met with a more favorable reception than might have been expected. Those sitting in judgment upon them were in reality enjoying themselves.

"Well, Doctor, what is your opinion?" the general turned to one of the officers.

The doctor merely tapped his forehead by way of answer.

And, in the upshot, after some discussion and considerable writing in sundry records, our heroes were released from any further military service.

"You are free to go now," they were informed. "You are herewith discharged."

Benjamin made a low bow as he took his departure.

Senderel, loyal as ever to his leader, marched off after him.